THE WILSON CHRONICLES

THE WILSON CHRONICLES

A Dog's Insight Into Humanity
&
Politics

Wilson

iUniverse, Inc.
New York   Bloomington

The Wilson Chronicles
A Dog's Insight Into Humanity & Politics

Copyright © 2007 by Wilson

All rights reserved. No part of this book may be used or reproduced by any means, graphic, electronic, or mechanical, including photocopying, recording, taping or by any information storage retrieval system without the written permission of the publisher except in the case of brief quotations embodied in critical articles and reviews.

This is a work of fiction. All of the characters, names, incidents, organizations, and dialogue in this novel are either the products of the author's imagination or are used fictitiously.

iUniverse books may be ordered through booksellers or by contacting:

iUniverse
1663 Liberty Drive
Bloomington, IN 47403
www.iuniverse.com
1-800-Authors (1-800-288-4677)

Because of the dynamic nature of the Internet, any Web addresses or links contained in this book may have changed since publication and may no longer be valid. The views expressed in this work are solely those of the author and do not necessarily reflect the views of the publisher, and the publisher hereby disclaims any responsibility for them.

ISBN: 978-0-595-48649-6 (sc)
ISBN: 978-0-595-60744-0 (ebook)

Printed in the United States of America

iUniverse rev. date: 11/16/2009

Contents

Foreword	ix
Rin Tin Tin &Communism	1
The Mailman	3
Birthday	6
Fascism	9
Lady And The Tramp	12
Ecuador	13
The Circus	16
The Quilting Circle	18
Evolution	21
Jackson Pollock	23
THE SHIT SHOW	26
Papal Indulgences	31
Bitch	32
The Language of Manipulation	34
Carmen Miranda	37
The Front Yard	40
T.V. Preachers & Other Weirdness	44
Sunlight	46

The Dalai Lama 48

Flock of Seagulls. 52

Letter from Todd 55

Hot Body. 57

Remorse. 60

Our Afghan Sisters. 61

Saint Patty's Day. 64

Pipe and Slippers 66

Doggie Style. 68

Breaking Thin Ice-The Gift. 74

The Dog Show 77

Hero Worship 80

The A List 82

Generation of The Doomed 85

Instant Karma 89

Epilogue 93

Post Epilogue—I Found Jimmy Hoffa 96

This Is Not A Fellini Movie 99

The Dixie Chicks Canines 101

Something/Anything 104

The Special Kibble 106

The Dinner Table. 109

The Key 113

J. Edgar Hoover & the Tea Party Girls 117

The Mortgage Crisis (let me get this straight) 123
Letter to My Publisher 124
The Road Too Much Traveled: The Interview 126
The Bus Trip: Go Greyhounds 129
GOD 133
Being Enlightened Doesn'tPlay Well in The Suburbs . . . 136

About Wilson and Daisy's Owner   141

Wilson T.

To KATHY & GEORGE,

Fondly,
Wilson
T.

Foreword

Hello, my name is Wilson T. and my wife's name is Daisy. We are both Boston Terriers. We reside with two adults, Todd and Bonnie and their two wonderful children, Aric and Beth. Through our years we have been observing humans and the politics that surround them. In general, canines as a species have tried to help change the status quo to a more level playing field for humans. What you are about to read is a chronological collection of letters from Daisy and I, which we have sent to Todd's relatives and friends whom we are close with. We tried to keep our insights concise, be politically relevant and remain humorous. In sharing our adventures and observations, we hope to inspire and also to help all understand our plight as well. Basically, having to cope with mankind and especially Todd.

Enjoy,
Wilson

Rin Tin Tin & Communism

I was thinking how indoctrinated we all are as a society. Numbed by propaganda via the media, a tool of this totalitarian dictatorship run by the ruling business class.

You didn't think dogs ponder and reflect on social politics did you? Well we do. One of us was even blacklisted in the 1950's for speaking out. Do you remember Rin Tin Tin? He was a famous German Sheppard who starred in his own television series. All Rin was trying to do was point out the differences between Communism and Capitalism. Communism, aside from the state sponsored terrorism and domestic spying, in theory was a good practice. Everybody receiving equal pieces of the economic pie, secured employment, housing, free health care, etc. In theory good: people not having to worry about stability could pursue loftier interests like philosophy. In practice though Communism never worked. The rich still wanted to maintain their level of wealth. The poor having apartments and jobs secured did not have a deeply ingrained work ethic. Hell, they couldn't even make toilet paper soft. (Which means a lot to anal, retentive morons, like my owner).

Capitalism on the other hand, aside from the state sponsored terrorism and domestic spying, is where the richest 1% own 95% of the wealth. Basically it's white slavery now, but it's called minimum wage. Which in fact is worse than the slavery of past centuries. There after a long hard days work, you would go back to your bunk and rest. Today after a long days work, you go home and worry about putting a life style together for $7.00 per hour.

That's all that Rin Tin Tin was trying to point out, but they shut him down anyway. You never saw him in movies again. Sure he worked as a part-time security guard dog, but the big time was over. The powers that be feared that he was going to wake a sleeping giant! Yes—the mindless propagandized American masses. Imagine if that apathetic wandering herd ever voted!

Daisy encourages me to speak out against social economic injustice, especially because we are Boston terriers from Boston, and have direct descendants to the Boston Tea Party. Remember no taxation without representation? Yea, that was us, but I'm tired of getting my head split open by the indoctrinated androids that defend the political machine.

Daisy on the other hand feels we should just kill the rich and feed them to the poor. Yes, but how rich is rich, and who decides? Not to mention moral and ethical issues. Daisy says morals and ethics are part of the cultural programming, a construct by who's in power, so they can stay in power. No, that's not the answer. Daisy wasn't taken for her afternoon walk that's just her repressed anger talking. There has to be some kind of order, rules that we can all agree on. One has to work within the structures established, through education, voting. It's, hold on. Daisy please come scratch my back, I can't reach it's between my shoulder blades. Aahhh that's it, thanks Daisy.

It's within our legal means, so we should try to bring about social and economic change for the greater good of all to have a more stable world, at least that was what old Rin's ideology was.

Wilson

The Mailman

I'm sitting here, having a bowl of rice; rice is great if you're hungry and want 2,000 of something. I'm waiting for the mailman to come. I nipped him last week and Todd wants me to apologize. What can I say; he startled me creeping up the front steps in his little blue shorts. He thinks he so cute too, just because he has thumbs.

Look at these teeth; these are not for eating vegetables. When the mailman comes, I'm like the great hunter perusing the savanna wetlands. He is like a gazelle ripe for the taking. You should see him run, throwing mail in the air, screaming. Anyway, I was told to make peace so we could receive mail again, so that's who, I'm waiting for.

I can barely see over the windowsill to see when he arrives. Nothing in this house is sized proportional for dogs. We're supposed to be man's best friend, they sure don't put out much effort. Some homes have doggie doors, but how degrading is that, having to crawl on my paws and knees. It would be nice having a doorknob low enough so I could turn it, oh yea, that opposable digit obstacle again. Do you have any idea how hard it is not being able to pick up stuff you want? Not to mention not having any pockets to put your stuff in. Every time I pass by something amazing like a chewed piece of bubblegum, I say great, it sure would be nice to take you home to chew later. Sure I get to sniff and lick, I'm just saying dogs can't collect stuff. I mean have you ever seen a dog with a collection of anything?

Not to mention not being able to reach the gas peddles on a car for a Sunday drive. You think I like being a passenger all the time, having to stick my head out of the window just to see. For once I would like to get behind the wheel and see if 350 horsepower is all that powerful? My money is still on the 350-greyhound power, dogs tried to make. Now that was car engine! Unfortunately it never got past the prototype stage do to lack of engineering and manufacturing. Dogs are just not that good with our hands as a species. Don't get me wrong, were specialized in many things, like tracking, those bloodhounds are incredible. German Shepard's at security, border collies at herding, not to mention Schnauzers at accounting and bookkeeping. We are amazing, but we just have no good woodworkers. We tried sub-contracting all the woodworking out to the Chimpanzees, but they kept goofing around too much.

Seriously, if you could build scaled down homes for dogs, well let's just say they'll be no poops on your lawn mister, we do know how to repay a favor.

Besides, have you seen the price of those crappy pre-manufac-tured doghouses lately? Housing has tripled in price in the last ten years. My wages have not tripled! What's going on? Fewer people can't afford these doghouses. Daisy says it's the government's way to manipulate and control the lower socio-economic classes. There she goes bringing classes into it again. Although, I don't know how our four kids are going to afford a home in ten years unless they're mortgaged to the hilt. I mean $375,000.00 for a two bed-room ranch home, when the average dog makes $25,000.00. (That's if he can find work. You do remember what happened to Rin Tin Tin)?

Hold on here comes the mailman. Hey! Mailman (bark bark), I want to apologize(bark), no don't run, please come back, don't throw the mail, please wait, come back(bark bark bark), I was going to serve espresso.

This is definitely not good. Did you ever have one of those days that went from bad to worse? How do you pick yourself up and turn it around? Well, I guess it's ones own subjective interpretation of their perception. I'll tell Todd-shit happens-lighten up! It's only mail baby booby bubby. It's not like it was something incredible like a chewed up piece of gum! Where are your priorities? Well, the kids should be home anytime now from school and I have to appear enthused and perky, oh the things I do for humanity. Plus I have to chase those damn squirrels out of the backyard again, they're always leaving their cigarette butts on the lawn.

So get back to me on that woodworking idea, ok?

Later,
Wilson

Oh yeah, that reminds me, did you ever get the cannolis that I sent with Todd last week? He probably ate them on the way. I don't know how you put up with him at times. Me, personally, I try to avoid him as much as possible.

Birthday

They told me I was supposed to decorate the tree, but they never told me I was going to be put on psychotropic kibble-those jerks. Man, am I high! I can hardly concentrate on putting the Christmas ornaments on the tree or myself, which is it again?

By the way did you know that dog spelled backwards is God? Kind of makes you think. I have these epiphanies that we are all one: dog, man, bird, etc., all connected as one heart, one mind. I look out the window and see a flock of geese all flying in unison. I see the unified field theory in one synergistic moment. I think I can fly.

Beth stands by me, she appears so transparent, translucent and yet she seems right next to me. "I am he as you are he as you are me and we are all together. See how they run like pigs from a gun see how they fly. I'm flying. Yellow matter custard dripping from a dead dogs eye. Cronalocker fishmark, stupid bloody Tuesday, man you should of seen them kicking Edgar Allen Poe. I am the egg man, they are the egg man, I am the walrus. Kuku ca Ju, kuku ca Ju, cu". (The Beatles).

Love,
Daisy

Hi, it's me Wilson. Beth put this party hat on my head to celebrate your birthday. The things I do for you. You better be having a good time and lots of fun, because I could be out chasing cats.

I snuck out a few weeks ago and had Todd chase me around the neighborhood for one whole hour! Have you ever seen a man of fifty plus years run for one hour? Man, what a hoot. To save face for him and not to get in trouble I ran under a S.U.V. and was tumbled around by the transmission. It was worth it though. Like I tell Todd you got to have some fun once and awhile: go out and bite a mailman. I enjoy the smell of flesh in the morning, at least that's what Robert Duvall's Doberman once told me. Though he's kind of whacked out from all those tours of K-9 duty in Viet Nam.

By the way, can you make your eyes go sideways like I can? I'll teach you the next time I see you. Excuse me for a moment … Daisy keeps mumbling something about a stream of consciousness. I don't know what the hells she's talking about. Now you see why I got to go out once and awhile? Every Friday night I get together with the guys for cigars and poker. Our buddy Van Gough; we call him that because he lost one ear in a car accident. Van's a German Shepherd who likes to paint and he's working on painting us on a black velvet canvas playing cards. Cool or what? I hear it's high art going to be worth a lot of money.

Listen, we should get together before I die in three to five years. Well that's twenty one to thirty five years in your time, but never the less a point well taken. So when you come visit, we could run around, play catch, sniff, scratch, stretch, it'll be fun. When I do see you though I will have to growl a bit just to keep up appearances.

Oh, I almost forgot, when you call if Todd answers hang up. I was supposed to be guarding the house, but instead went to a 3Dog Night concert where I met a couple of French poodles. Well one thing led to another and I didn't come home for a few days. Daisy's real upset so I'm lying low. Keep in touch.

Wilson

P.S. Did you know that bowling is mans oldest sport? Yea, it dates back to when you only had three fingers!

Fascism

What the hell is going on over there? We send Todd over for a visit, and he comes home ranting about the wonders of Fascism. Granted, I could see if you wanted to run a country, where the towns and municipalities functioned in a productive and efficient way for all concerned, like getting the trains to run on time, great!

When it comes to collectively bundling our intellect and thinking under one glorious dictating leader, that's where I draw the line. I am a self realized, enlightened being, who just happens to be in the form of what you refer to as a dog, in this particular incarnation. Get it? I'm serious you don't know how bad it is, Todd's gone off the deep end, we now have to wear our underwear on the outside of our clothes! I mean now really, that is a bit much. We used to be a nice autonomous collective where decisions were made by a simple majority regarding internal affairs, and a two-thirds majority regarding external affairs. Quite frankly were having second thoughts on sending him over for future visits. You know how impressionable he is. Enclosed is a photo "the shoe store incident" just before he was asked to leave for harassing customers. Ever since, he's been in lockdown 24/7. We only let him out to visit you because we know you'll look after him and keep an eye on him.

Daisy (D):	Wilson, what are you doing?
Wilson (W):	I'm writing a letter to our cousin Lenny.
D:	Yes, but you're sounding rude, that's no way to start a letter, especially to your cousin.
W:	That's my point, he is my cousin I can feel free to say how I feel with out recriminations.
D:	I'm just saying you should just rethink what you said in another way.
W:	There you go, this is the very same thing I'm complaining about, "Il Duce" bag. You trying to dictate and oppress me with your version of what I should be thinking. Next you'll be having me pledge allegiance to symbols to further control and manipulate my thoughts, all under the guise of freedom, you scoundrel.
D:	Wilson, I think you are over reacting. I'm just saying your letters a bit rude. When is the last time you told your cousin you loved him, instead of writing a nasty letter?
W:	It's not nasty for Christ's sake. Happy now, you just threw off the whole tone of the letter I had going. Ok Len & Nancy I love you, happy now Daisy, now stop bothering me.
D:	What you said didn't sound like you meant it. You just said I love you, to appease me.
W:	Get out; get out!

Seriously, I'm tired of wearing my underwear on the outside. I look ridiculous; the chipmunks are starting to snicker, not to mention the new memo about goose-stepping. You need to have a talk with him soon, promise me.

Give my best to your cat, Pouh; I've always been in awe of how detached, cool, calm, and collected she is from the material world, like a Zen Master. Actually her genetics precede Zen; she dates back to the pyramids.

Wilson.

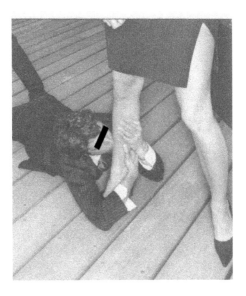

The Shoe Store Incident

Lady And The Tramp

I'm sitting reclined in the black leather lazy-boy chair smoking a cigar. Daisy is in the kitchen making sauce. When we know the family is going out for eight to ten hours we like to stretch out and relax. Daisy makes a great sauce; she starts with a can of tomato paste, a couple of cans of tomato puree, then a basil leaf. I can't say too much more because it is her Aunt Rita's secret recipe and Daisy took a vow of death never to revile the recipe.

When the pasta is ready were going to watch Lady and the Tramp. That's why I'm writing, to tell you it is a wonderful movie that I think you would enjoy. Daisy likes the part where the two dogs kiss while sharing spaghetti. We like when art imitates real life. Besides, the movie reminds us of when we were younger. We were quite romantic. You wouldn't think it now, being that I let myself go, due to doggie treat addiction, but when we were younger we were quite the couple.

When we're through, we make sure everything is cleaned up by the time the family comes home, except for the lingering cigar smoke in the air. Bonnie thinks Todd's been smoking in the house again and he catches holy hell, man its great!

You never got back to me if you received the cannolis that I sent with Todd last month.

Later,
Wilson

Ecuador

It's been awhile since I last wrote. Daisy and I went to visit our friends Chi Chi and Peaches. They're a Chihuahua couple who live in the Ecuadorian forest. We had a wonderful time. Chi Chi and Peaches are a lot of fun, real carefree. The hospitality was great and the food stupendous; spicy is not the word! I had a dish that was flavored with habanero peppers. They should be pronounced "Ha You Been Dared Oh!" Let's just say when I go to the bathroom I spit thunder and crap lightening.

Chi Chi was saying that life has been difficult for the indigenous native tribes, who make up ninety percent of the population. It appears that billion dollar companies from the U.S.A., via help from the C.I.A. cajole the ruling class, the one percent of the population into building dams for electric power. This helps the ruling one percent maintain their level of wealth and power. In turn, the building of the dams and the aftermath destroy the natural habitats that the local population needs to survive: fishing, hunting, plants and vegetation. Whole tribal populations are displaced. Streams polluted by soil runoff because trees have been cut down. There is a real eco-disaster going on right now!

It turns out that a U.S. company built the dam, so now Ecuador is in debt for billions of dollars plus interest. Many suffer while the few prosper. History shows that technically advanced cultures dominate the less technical. This is an unfair, unjust system. Will humans ever wake up to realize that we are all interconnected and their actions eventually affect themselves as well?

Aside from corporate greed, human insanity and thousands of oil byproduct waste ponds left by TEXACO because it was more cost effective to not put the waste back deep into the earth. These oil waste ponds seep into and pollute the water table. We still had a wonderful time. There are still a few natural untouched places that Chi Chi and Peaches took us to that were breathtaking. The beauty and wonder of nature, of life itself amazes me. Chi' Chi and Peaches are part of a grass roots movement to slow the destruction so future generations can survive.

While we were vacationing we let our friend Dana take over our security duties for Todd and family. Dana is real nice; he is an older, retired Great Dane. His wife Trudy recently passed away. Although Dana is still in mourning, we thought that keeping him engaged in life by guarding our home would be a good idea.

Trudy was a great dog. She was a tall, big poodle, like Aunt Helens dog Dino. Trudy was real classy, she made you feel welcomed, always said the right words to make you feel comfortable. She just passed away one night in her sleep from old age. Time just has its way. It happens eventually to all of us unfortunately. I think it's in our understanding and acceptance of death that we get to better know ourselves within the big picture of Creation.

Dana won't remarry it's not in his nature. He's been with Trudy since the beginning of time itself; he will always honor her memory. Dana has a lot of friends to lift his spirits if necessary. He also volunteers one day a week at the homeless dog shelter.

I'll never forget how Daisy and I met Dana and Trudy. We were taking a stroll in the park and Dana and Trudy were playing catch with a Frisbee. I thought I would try and be cool and impress Daisy with my leaping ability and grab their Frisbee in mid flight. Instead I tripped full speed into Dana and was knocked unconscious. Needless to say when I came to Dana wasn't impressed, being that he too was in pain. Fortunately for me Dana understood my youthful exuberance. Trudy and Daisy quickly became friends and the whole "Frisbee incident" was forgotten. We double dated many times. Trudy's passing was hard on Daisy as well, they were close, they shared dog food recipes, sat in the sun together. Generally, they just enjoyed each other's company. So now you could see why we wanted to keep Dana somewhat engaged by guarding our home. Dana did a great job too, by the way. He kept the squirrels in line; they're always leaving their cigarette butts on the lawn. Yet he let the chipmunks play on the sod. This in itself was quite a task.

He got on well with Todd and the family. Dana and Todd look a lot alike with the droopy eyes. You don't know if they're stoned or have been up all night. The same long face, Todd has this King Arthur round table beard going on now. Daisy thinks he looks awful, like an old white owl.

We're back home now and the transition was smooth. You can also write to us now that my lawyer settled our negotiations with Todd. Yea, he has to pay me one dollar per week in our profit sharing agreement!

Until then,
Wilson

The Circus

Daisy and I just came back from the circus. We had a great time. My master Todd (wow what a oxymoron that is) said the only way we can go is if we work the camera, oh for joy.

There was this Shriner's circus in town. They do a lot of wonderful charitable work for burn victims, especially children. They're also the guys that crawl up inside your mind at night and mess with your head while you're dreaming. The other day I mooned a guy for no apparent reason, it turns out to be Todd's accountant. Just last week I found myself leaving a flaming bag of my own dog doo on some ones front porch and it wasn't even Halloween, this time it turns out to be Todd's lawyer. So something is definitely going on for sure. Anyway when we got there, Todd flashed the gate man a secret hand sign and we were in like Flynn. This was cool because it was my turn to pay.

We had a ball, we rode elephants, ate cotton candy, the whole nine yards. I asked Todd what was his favorite act? He said the half naked sweaty female trapeze artist, being that she reminds him of a warm Florida beach this time of year. Todd then asked me what my favorite act was. (Todd actually showed an active interest in my feelings and opinions). Daisy said he just gives you the illusion that he cares. Anyway my favorite act was this: A guy comes on stage, center ring, and gets a prostrate exam, all while he does his own taxes. Such focus and concentration it was amazing!

We liked the circus so much Daisy and I went back stage to talk to the owner about an old vaudevillian comedy act we have been working on, to actually bring to life on the circus stage. He tells us to describe the act. Well I tell him, first we come out on stage, then I start humping Daisy, when that's over we then pee on the first three rows of audience, then take a bow.

He says: that's quite an act! What do you call yourselves? I say: "The Aristocrats".

Wilson

The Quilting Circle

You have been on my mind a lot and I have been meaning to write but I've been busy lately. The past few months I've been taking in laundry to try and save some money. Wilson and I would like to leave eventually and be on our own. We have a circus act we've been working on and I think we are ready to take it on the road. It's difficult to have loyalty to Todd after knowing that he sold our children. What kind of a culture in-doctrines people to have such belief systems that selling other species is ok? It's not only our species they do it to, other species as well. Some are even killed and eaten! I feel I'm living on a planet of ghouls and vampires.

Enclosed is a photo of our three offspring, two girls and one boy. Fortunately I still get to see one of my daughters from that litter and another daughter from our second.

The other day Todd apologized for selling our offspring. He admitted that he now knows the pain of loosing a child to this sick and twisted culture we are trapped in. Video games for the boys to prolong adolescence and keep them out of the political arena. Also oversexed fashion for the girls, cultural child abuse at best. Emotionally it's difficult for him to see his children get wrapped up in the media, the music, fashion, advertising, schools, institutions, in general: the rat race. He feels this current culture drains their true spirit and humanity out of them. Being exposed to all of the cultures distractions is like running ones head through a tree shredder. (I know, I've seen Entertainment Tonight).

I tell Todd to lighten up. All things must pass, all things must pass away. His children are smart enough to see through the propaganda and indoctrination and besides how else are they going to truly know what real crap is unless exposed to our culture. Besides, what about all those nature walks you took them on? I think that's why Todd loved Pleasant Beach so much, it gave him the illusion that he was on a tropical island with the sand dunes and lush vegetation. Trees, water, sunshine, nature, have a way about bringing one to find beauty and truth. These are the life affirming vibratory energies that sustain our spirits.

Look at him mumbling, just a shell of his former self, pathetic, sad really. Ever since the beach house was sold Todd's been coping with existential issues, lets just say it's a process, he'll get there. That's why I don't know if we really are going to leave him. Todd, Wilson and I are all in the same boat. We've all lost so much.

I have to go now that my washing cycle is done. When you come visit maybe you would like to join the girls and me? On Thursday evenings we get together for a quilting circle. We all contribute to making a quilt, and discuss overthrowing the government and the institutions that enslave us as a species by helping them change their awareness, consciousness and viewpoint of their conception of reality. One day they may just walk away from it all and decide to not be the person they have been projecting into time and space, to quiet their politics of oppression. Humans do have epiphanies. It is quite empowering to get together and sew as one mind. Although the groups not the same since Trudy passed on.

Love,
Daisy

research, bridge building, electricity, music, the dewy decimal system, you get the drift? Though humans are evolving at different rates and there are many, with money who are not so benevolent. These are the humans who control, suppress others and force their subjective view of reality onto them. What the hell do I know though? I'm just a dog with a collar around my neck, chained by a leash tied to a poll, trapped by the human mind that is still evolving. Boy, what I would give for a sock, filled with manure and opposable thumbs to start swinging it.

Listen, when you come visit, could you bring some bolt cutters?

Thanks,
Wilson

The Wilson Chronicles

Jackson Pollock

Did you know that one of Todd's favorite painters is Jackson Pollock? The reason is because Jackson's agent was able to sell his creations as art. It turns out that old Jackson's alcohol induced creative rants via paint and canvas, made it into the collective conscious archives as art. Go figure, who would have guessed? Well it seems that if you have a concept and turn it into an idea with philosophical jargon attached, fueled by an agent with advertising, you get Abstract Expressionist Painting. So that's what they call a bunch of splattered paint on canvas these days. Please don't misunderstand me I know Jackson's heart and mind were in the right place, that he was sincere in his search for truth and beauty evolving into a new form of meaningfulness.

I get it. Though it still amazes me that you can label one painters work art, like Da Vinci's, work that reflects an image exactly, as well as Pollock's spattering. It's in how you define art, and the politics that slowly slip it into the general public's awareness to eventually become part of the culture.

I personally like to see the artist paint an exact image of something before he goes abstract and is bestowed the title Art, rather than kindergarten finger-paint. Call me old school; call me an indoctrinated android from the culturally elite of ages past. It's just that before Jackson came along the advertising propaganda machine had done its job too well. They convinced me so deeply, now my programming won't cognize a new construct as Pollock's work as art. Sad really. I think that is why it brings Todd so much happiness to look at a Jackson Pollock painting, because he does see the freedom of the artist's intent and he smiles at the inventiveness of the political linguistics that brought it into the forefront to be recognized.

So with all that in mind, that is why I am writing. Something extraordinary recently happened. About a week ago the front door was left open to air out the house. Then out of what appeared to be nowhere, ran in Alvin Squeaky Fromme Squirrel (no relation to the cartoon chipmunk or the immoral delusional paranoid from the Manson family). Alvin is a squirrel, one of the ringleaders who throws his cigarette butts on our lawn. I thought to myself it's just you and me now, its payback time rodent. We ripped into each other like a mother into self-esteem, his pack of lucky strikes dropping out of his pockets. Damn, he has pockets and I don't, I thought to myself as we tussled for our lives on the wooden floor. Blood, fur, mud, dirt, and skin were flying everywhere. Did I mention blood? It seemed to be spraying all over the place. Blood spattered on the walls, the couch, and the ceiling. Right in the middle of this roughhouse rampage I saw it; the living room looked like one giant Jackson Pollock painting. My jaw dropped in awe of this spontaneous montage homage to Jackson Pollock. I saw it for the first time, this creative flow that reflected the conscious and unconscious state of mind I had been in, powerful indeed. Needless to say during my catatonic like stunned amazement Alvin had long since run off to fight another day.

I thought to myself what better gift to Todd than to share this piece of artwork and my newfound appreciation of abstract expressionism with him. Knowing Todd he may even put a frame around this magnificence.

Well, when Todd arrived home I could see that he was in awe. His face color turned to a whiter shade of pale, then his eyes started to bug out like mine, almost to the point of popping out of his skull. I thought how cool is that! He's probably going to congratulate me, maybe even buy me a higher grade of kibble. Not like the psychoactive dog food they feed Daisy, although she now understands quantum physics and sub-atomic particle movement.

The next thing I know is I get kicked outside, tied to a leash, chained to a pole. What the hell gives? I've had it with these temperamental artists, damn ingrate. That's the last time I try to show him a good time via the medium of creative expression.

Thanks for the invite though, but I'm too sad to come over and play with the new squeaky plastic hamburger you bought; besides I'm chained to a pole by a human mind once again.

> I'll call you,
> Wilson

THE SHIT SHOW

I was thinking about ones perspective of life. I think, how one interprets the phenomenal world is a subjective viewpoint that defines their reality. Take depression for instance, it's a concept, an idea to attempt to articulate ones mood, ones state of mind, ones reaction and interpretation of their perception of an event. If an organic brain disorder is ruled out, then depression usually represents some loss, something that did not turn out the way the person wanted it to.

The Roman Philosopher Seneca, basically said don't expect much and you won't be disappointed. (Was Seneca a step ahead of Buddha? Being that Buddha said, "life is suffering", not, it's the way you interpret an event that's causing you suffering). In all fairness to Buddha though he did have a wonderful eight fold path to enlightenment, and besides he was referring to not being attached to anything, being that it was in time and would pass away eventually. In theory similar to Seneca, not being attached to an outcome or a point of view could be interpreted to mean when you expect nothing you will not be disappointed with a certain outcome. Especially when you take into consideration factors of random probability. I'm digressing, non-the less.

It's how one interprets an event, how one categorizes the event in his or her own mind. For example: two soldiers in war see their friend get his head blown off. One soldiers develops Post Traumatic Stress Disorder (PTSD), the other does not.

It's all how you interpret your perception of what happens, that's what I tell Todd. He says I'm being indoctrinated by the new semantics the politically correct are pushing these days. Man, he really hates psychologists, therapists of any kind (he should know, he's one himself). Very, very few therapies such as cognitive/behavioral have scientific empirical evidence behind them. Most therapies have no statistically significant validity. That means picking your nose, or receiving a swift kick in the butt has just as much probability for a positive clinical outcome as the therapy your being sold. (So that's why he has a big boot in his office, I've always wondered about that). He thinks most therapists haven't enough wisdom, nor comprehend the human mind's relationship with the Universe in all its multidimensional ramifications. Most therapists are charlatans and full of crap, especially that sexually repressed freak Sigmund Freud, who projected his neuroses onto women. What do you expect from a cocaine addict? He made his fame on only six case studies. Freud's idea of the Id, Ego and the Super Ego, now that's creative writing! Graduate school though, that's where the real indoctrination and propaganda occurs Todd says. Who else are the ruling class going to get to control the minds of the masses. There are the police for behavioral issues and graduate school for propaganda.

The worst are MDs and psychiatrists that prescribe anti-psychotic medication for misdiagnosed mental disorders in children. This is cultural child abuse, driven and fueled by a multi-billion dollar pharmaceutical industry. They're all on the gravy train, rather than teach better parenting skills to the parents. The lower socioeconomic strata of our society are the new genie pigs. There are no long-term studies, no scientific validity. This is an abomination. Morons with diplomas that haven't a clue about the human psyche. Crimes against our most precious resource, our children.

Aside from being a licensed Psychotherapist, Todd has a Post-Graduate Degree in Homeopathic Medicine from London England. He's licensed to practice in Ontario Canada. The American Medical Association (AMA) has applied political pressure, so now it's illegal to practice Homeopathy in New York State. Not that Todd would want to anyway. He says that there are no original molecules from the original tincture base past 12c. As the medicine gets stronger, you keep diluting it, eventually to a certain point (12c) where there are no original molecules left from your original herb/flower tincture base. Now that's bordering on the mystical, magical beliefs to sell a gullible, naive public. Where's the empirical evidence, the high validity research with water memory transfer rather than a bias philosophical discourse to sway my viewpoint. That is why Todd doesn't practice. I don't think he really believes too much in Homeopathy either. I think I'm starting to see why Todd doesn't believe much in anything anymore, why he's a recluse, well other than the Seraphims that visit him. I think the last one was Metatron.

It's sad really. I might be that way too if I thought that my academic career was a waste of time and money. When one sees through their occupation and its modalities and transcends them, it's difficult to go back and practice especially with a straight face. He says it's all a shit show, a real dog and pony shit show. Personally I'm offended. I don't know why he has to bring dogs into this?

I tell Todd the trick in this shit show (pay attention) is to expect nothing from life, like his philosopher buddy Seneca. Bring it down to zero, then start there. Appreciate the single blade of grass, like a Zen Master. When you get through that epiphany, move on to trees, to birds, to dogs (I threw myself in there for poetic license), the miracle of sunlight, to oneself, to the unity and wonder of each other. It's all there in your garden, if one looks deep enough.

Just don't get caught up on the propaganda of the shit show other people are peddling. There will always be unenlightened humans who want to oppress, enslave and control others with their viewpoint. (I mean growing humans from carbon molecules is really no exact science. You did come from monkeys. You are evolving at different rates; let's just say these United States are not that united.) The religious right, and the new age left will be peddling their dogma, their belief systems for money. President Bush will be peddling war under the guise of protecting you against some new boogieman, for the sake of freedom and democracy, all while the people who put him in power get rich selling guns and oil.

I know it's a fine line here, because all of what I just said here is my interpretation of the phenomenal world. My subjective viewpoint could just be considered as another grain of sand on the beach along with the shit show. I feel I'm closer to the mystery of the who, the where and why of life, than say a Carney huckster outside a Las Vegas showroom calling you in. One never knows though, and besides taking a rest from the shit show to appreciate a great set of legs is a welcomed relief. Then again that is part of the shit show. It's basically an enigma, rapped into a conundrum, masked again as a mystery within an enigma.

Todd says, "My brain is working overtime and that's how I got the googol eyes. He tells me to turn on, tune in and drop out, and marginalize myself to the fringes of society, like he has. Like a Taoist monk, go back to nature and find God and let this current culture pass by and erode like all the others, (now there's a community builder). Of course help out in the moment when you can, after all, we are just

God having a conversation with himself, or herself if you're a feminist. He says what's the alternative, mindless, soulless capitalism? Money, greed, secret agendas, shiny sparkling things? Power? One is a lost soul wasting time with these pursuits".

Hey! I like shiny sparkling things, and besides all this doesn't mean much, coming from a guy with the letter R and L stamped on his shoes. Todd says the R represents right wing conservatism and the L is for left wing liberal, which are both a metaphor to always remember that one must walk the narrow middle path between the two like a razors edge to find balance and truth. I ask myself should I be paying attention or is he just messing with my head as he usually does with his philosophical jargon. The other day he tells me that every three out of four people make up seventy five percent of the population. You see what I mean? He's driving me nuts, not to mention that I'm the one with the collar on, enslaved. Although he does plant trees, and is kind to chipmunks.

I've got to go, those damn squirrels are smoking cigarettes in the backyard again; they're always leaving their butts on the lawn. ------------------Later, Wilson.

Papal Indulgences

The reason I am writing is to mention that when you do go visit Italy, do not forget to visit the sixteenth chapel. No not the sis teen chapel, the 16th. This is a small chapel with a ceiling that Pope Julius also commissioned Michelangelo to do, but never mind that. What you really need to check out is the side bathroom there. Pope Brochette commissioned the renaissance artist Angelo Graffiti to do the ceiling. It's incredible, such articulation and verbosity. There are passages about worldly travelers from Kent and Nantucket, others that have sat and are broken hearted. Check it out.

Oh! Speaking of the guise of selling papal indulgences to get into heaven to pay for the commissioned ceiling. I could sell you some Papal doggie indulgences and favors for a price. For $ 49.95 these doggie favors guarantee you, that when you do go to heaven you won't have any dog crap on your shoes from the shit show!

Think about it and get back to me,
Wilson

BITCH

I thought I'd drop you a line. I haven't written in awhile and a few things have been on my mind. Hold on. Daisy's mumbling something to me, something about how the government uses the concept of democracy to indoctrinate the poor to go to war. Yea, yea, yea Daisy I heard it all before Noam Chomsky good, the ruling class bad. Ok I get it, do you mind I'm trying to write a letter here.

Sorry about that, anyway like I was saying. Wait a minute; I don't think I even started yet. That's how crazy Daisy makes me, trying to distract me most of the time with her issues.

Anyway, like I was trying to say … Stop, Daisy!

Daisy just ran off with my pen. Yes I'm writing with my second pen, but she took my favorite pen. Her hormones are all over the place lately. First she wants to play then she doesn't want to, then she does. I think Daisy is going through a change of life. No she is too young. Maybe her behavior is because our kids have grown up and left the nest?

Daisy's always used to mothering. I think she is just trying to adjust to her new concept of herself. I try to tell her that she is an infinite spiritual being, that there is no lost connection just an unfolding of oneself from one moment to the next.

Then the next thing I know is we're not humping, she's not even speaking to me, go figure! One must choose ones words wisely I'm starting to realize.

Well, that's what brings me to why I'm writing. My buddy Ralphie, a Yorkshire terrier who lives down the road heard his master call his wife a bitch. Then she whacked him upside the head with a frying pan. Ralphie's hanging out until the atmosphere cools down.

Apparently semantics change meaning from species to species. When I call Daisy a bitch I'm just referring to her female gender. Sometimes I use an international flair to be cool and say Be-ach.

So that's why I'm writing, to warn you whatever you say, never ever call a female in your species a bitch or you could wind up like Ralphie's owner with one side of your head caved in. Although Ralphie says his owner now picks up F.M. radio stations. It's not worth the gamble.

Hold on, I got some hamburgers on the grill I need to flip … Ok I'm back. Today I'm cooking burgers for the family. Well they think that there burgers. Let's just say the Henderson's Ferret won't be burrowing holes in our lawn anymore.

A better lawn, for a better tomorrow,
Later,

Wilson

The Language of Manipulation

Thanks for sending me your comments about the book that you just finished, "War and Peace". You know, you are one of the few humans who actually respond to my letters. I have a policy that I never read a book that weighs more than I do, though I definitely sympathize with your views. Yes, war is hell. My heart aches when I hear that a K-9 soldier has died. I think of the sadness and trauma one bullet caused to parents, wives, and children. Lives and destinies forever changed. You know this first hand, you were once part of the Military complex.

Unlike the real danger of World War II, recently our government led the country to believe that we were in eminent danger of attack, through the manipulation of language. This was accomplished by flaunting ideological concepts like democracy and freedom. This mostly a rouse to hide a secret agenda of taking another country's natural resources, and have a foothold in that region for the future. Many human lives are lost.

What of the soldiers that survive? Both sides were taught to believe what they did was right, and for their country. The government even imposed meaning and legitimacy to sanction killing again with language, to shiny sparkling medals and awarded them to justify the soldier's actions.

Many brave, honorable soldiers feel that they have been lied to, and taken advantage of. A pawn trapped and manipulated into believing a bunch of words that don't mean much anymore, especially to the soldiers that killed many. In their heart they know that in any other circumstance they would go to jail for murder and possibly be labeled a psychotic. Though because of some words they now are called hero. Killing is killing no matter what; a cultures ideology justifying murder does not change the fact. The soldier feels the burden, suffers and knows war is hell. Please don't misunderstand me, I know there are really bad people out there believing that killing the innocent still justifies their cause and we really do have to go fight them but it doesn't cost a trillion dollars! Instead of using the government's high-tech toys to also spy on its own people, how about spending the taxpayer's money on infrastructure so I can get around? Fix some bridges.

All these recent wars were against countries that do not even pose an eminent danger to us, where were those weapons of mass destruction again? What about a silent enemy that's real and kills Americans and Canadians? Tobacco kills over 500,000 Americans and Canadians every single year, also millions more throughout the world. Do you think that the public would be outraged to know, or do you think they would be pacified by the manipulation of language into compliancy? Why isn't the government taking action against the tobacco fields of our South and sending in the Marines where tobacco is grown and owned by multibillion dollar multinational corporations? At least go after those high priced, drug dealing pharmaceutical companies that have a monopoly over our elderly. Is the answer self-evident or am

I being redundant? It's just not good for big business, which basically use our government to do their bidding.

You see what happens when dog owners send their dogs to school? You're at home thinking that we're learning how to walk on a leash; instead we're burning the midnight oil reading political manifestos. Education is a good thing; it helps level the playing field, providing you haven't sold out. I've got to go Todd's calling me. I have to pretend to show him how I learned how to walk on a leash at "doggie training class".

Semper Fi
Wilson

Carmen Miranda

Wilson, (W): Damn it!

Daisy, (D): You're going to wake the family with that banging. What's the matter?

W: I hit my paw with the hammer trying to hang my picture of Carmen Miranda, son of a gun that hurts!

D: I don't like when you swear, you sound so rude and uncouth, besides, what are you doing with that silly old picture?

W: For your information Miss Manners, Carmen Miranda gave fruit to all the K9s in World War II. It's out of her selfless, kind act that I pay homage to her in the form of this picture. Isn't she beautiful with that pineapple, banana, and assorted fruit on her head?

D: Wait a minute World War II was no wear near Brazil.

W: Well a fight broke out in one of the neighborhoods over some of her records, and the K-9s were sent in. Happy now? For Christ's sake!

D: There you go again with the swearing. I'm beginning to think your story is all a rouse for you to hang a picture of Carmen Miranda?

W: No way.

D: You're as mendacious as a cat on a hot tin roof professing a chill. Why don't you just admit the fact that you have a thing for Carmen Miranda?

W: Leave me alone.

D: Wilson, I saw you humping the photo!

W: I had an itch I needed to scratch; can't a dog have a moment of privacy and scratch in peace?

D: What, I don't satisfy you enough, and you have to go about in the dead of night humping pictures like some drooling perverted mongrel degenerate.

W: I'm telling you I had an itch and all I did was scratch myself.

D: This isn't going to be like the time you had a thing for Esther Williams and you walked around in a Speedo all day long, is it?

W: You know, one more obscure reference and you're going to loose the audience.

D: Ah go screw yourself you lying rat bastard!

W: Oh that's rich, Ms. Manners.

The Front Yard

Daisy (D): What in the world are you doing?

Wilson (W): What do you think I'm doing, I'm sniffing the dog poop on our front yard.

D: That's disgusting.

W: What do you mean? I'm a dog, that's how I find out information, my old factory senses, relaying information to my brain.

D: You sick perverted bastard. You'll say anything to get a sniff of feces.

W: No, seriously, I'm just checking it out. My nose says Ralph and Betty have been by.

D: What, They can't scratch at the door and say hello like normal dogs?

W: I don't think they came by to visit.

D: Are you saying they came three blocks away from there home, dodging traffic, in this heat, just to take a crap on our lawn?

W: I'm not saying anything. I'm just pointing out that Ralph and Betty have been by. I don't know the circumstances.

D: Of all the nerve, that's it, that's the last time we are visiting them! I never did like going over to Betty's home anyway. She still keeps the plastic wrap on, that came with her furniture when it was delivered. The plastic sticks to my bottom.

W: Ralph's got a bladder condition.

D: We're not going.

W: Hey, don't drag me into this. Ralph and Betty are my close friends.

D: Yes, I think a little too close. I thought something was up when you immediately knew it was Betty's scent. You've been sniffing a little bit to close I suspect.

W: Quit being paranoid. I just came out to the front yard to stretch and sniff around, and I get all this drama? It's eight o'clock in the morning!

D: I'm not speaking to you, Mr. Casanova.

W: Good, you're giving me a headache.

D: We're not hanging out with the super wealthy anymore, just the moderately wealthy. They are shallow, all they value is their shiny objects and they judge each other by all the stuff they have acquired.

Boy, would I love to give them 250mg. of my kibble and have them see the light. Don't get me wrong, I do like them, they mean well, but they're like lost judgmental children searching. They identify with material objects, especially Betty with her diamond-studded collar. With their inane conversation, they are a drain to be around, plus they soiled our lawn, or did you forget that Mr. Olfactory senses?

W: I thought you said you weren't talking to me? We should accept other dogs on an individual basis, are we any more advanced with all our bickering? Maybe you're just jealous? Besides, every dog has their own journey of truth and self-discovery in this lifetime to grow through, just like those crazy humans. Do not interfere with Ralph and Betty's free will, soul development, or they're cosmic destiny. Remember, we are souls incarnate in the material world, life is a spiritual journey coupled of course with our true purpose of expelling carbon dioxide for the crabgrass.

D: For once I may actually agree to you.

W: What about the effect you may be having on them? Oh compassionate, empathic one, friendship is a two-way street you know. You can dish it out, but can you take it?

D: That's it, I'm not speaking to you I'm going inside to play with my own squeaky toy.

W: Ah, the peace and quiet returns and once again I bask in nature's serene beauty.

Wilson & Daisy

T.V. Preachers & Other Weirdness

Should I even bother to comment about them? Is it even necessary? Is there any ground that hasn't been covered? They're still on

T.V. though, bilking the naive elderly out of their life savings. Haven't the laws of karmic retribution infected them with syphilitic sores and locus by now?

A snake oil salesman version of the spiritual universe combined with financial donations; can I just throw up right now?

Man, I have to get Todd to subscribe to a better cable package. How about some Lassie or Rin Tin Tin? I forgot the ruling class will not put on old reruns of Rin. Ok, how about some cartoons like Wonder Dog or The Banana Bunch? I'd settle for Huckleberry Hound. Anything rather than this evangelistic Dogma, no pun intended.

There's hardly any programming on TV of any relevance to the true human spirit. There's just weird fillers to distract you and they call it entertainment. My generation was the first to experience the medium of television and its programming. Shows then had relevance and meaning to humanity, shows like Playhouse 90, Steve Allen and Jack Paar. Also there was journalism that was hard hitting, that tried to get to the heart of the matter. Does anyone remember Edward R. Murrow? He'd be rolling over in his grave now if he saw what the programming has become. The new generation does not know this, they think TV's weirdness is normal.

The ruling business class has used the medium of television to water down human intelligence. The bulk of humanity, the viewer, has become irrelevant to the political process. You have been marginalized. You thought TV programming was a reflection of human life, it's a fictitious reflection. TV has become an abomination, a surrealistic journey to cloud your mind. It is just a way to keep 300 million Americans from actually maturing and becoming politically aware. Come on wake up! Before 9/11, Anne Heche's emotional problems were the big TV news, now it's Britney Spears' emotional/behavioral problems. Talk about your cruelty to animals. I know what, I'm going to exercise my free will while I still have it and shut the TV off and go sit in the sunlight.

Goodnight and good luck,
Wilson T

Sunlight

As I bask in the sunlight I am reminded, like the ancient Egyptians how wonderful light is, in all its miraculous vibratory power. Sunlight warms my little tush, sooths my muscles and eases my weary mind. Sunlight heals, nurtures, and sustains my spirit. Speaking of spirit, my home is where my spirit goes and now it goes to the sunlight.

Remember my fellow canines, that we are still mans best friend and when their technologies start to crash around them as the nature of time changes and shifts we will be there with compassion and wisdom to guide the way. To help all species unite into a new world. In the meantime remember to keep voting.

Love,
Wilson

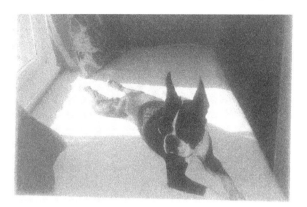

The Dalai Lama

You humans are something else. Every time someone comes along and starts to express the universal galactic message of peace, love and understanding, they get whacked. What's so funny about that? Incredible really. Mahatma Gandhi, Martin Luther King, Bobby Kennedy, John Lennon. Many, many more from other cultures too. Mother Teresa was spared because she was "the famous spiritual woman". It just wouldn't play well in the world press to have her whacked, even when she embarrassed the Pope by raising money for the poor by selling a Mercedes benz that the Pope gave her. It's not like she was some drug addict musician, cosmic messenger like Jim Morrison, Brian Jones, Janis Joplin, Jimmie Hendrix, the list goes on. Did the powers that be step in when China rolled into Tibet, crushing its culture, no of course not, it wouldn't be good for business. President Bush gives the Dalai Lama a shinny sparkly medal that mean some words, definitely not land. If President Bush thought so much of the Deli Lama, why wouldn't he manipulate China into returning Tibetan land to its rightful owners, the Tibetan People? Why, because it's just not good for business. China does own two trillion in United States Treasury bills. Are the dark forces of the underworld that potent around this little orb in space called earth, that the messengers of truth are being curtailed, stunted in every generation?

The Dalai Lama 49

Of ages past this phenomenon was linked to the devil. Those were dark times when the masses were ignorant, before the light of day had illuminated ones mind. Now I think it's big business using middle management (the Government) to do its bidding.

Are humans that lazy to not stand up and empower themselves? Once they take a stand, the willfully obedient press demonizes them. In the past the people's power was divided to be conquered. Is it the Builderberg Group, the Carlyle Group, the Trilatteral Commission? Who?

Is it something more sinister? Is it our feline friends the cats? Maybe it's the Doberman pinchers; they are a psychotic bunch genetically pumped up on steroid like adrenalins. The Dobermans were always thought to be the Benedict Arnolds of our species just because of their peculiar psychoses. The Universe has a way of balancing out itself though by giving us the Saint Bernard, their kegs of brandy always came in handy. Not to mention particular dogs like Opi and Max, a supreme like blend of Saint Bernard and Labrador Retriever and King Eimiller, the great German Shepard who saved my grandmother.

Listen, dogs as a species can only do so much. I mean, come on we don't even have opposable digits, you know thumbs. Do you expect me to actually try to pick up the sword? I can't even pick up the mighty pen. I'm lucky to be able to tap out these letters on my keyboard for Christ sakes! Don't count on Todd for that matter, he's lost in his own existential world of meaninglessness, isolation, freedom, control and death, and that's just his issues with having to sit through the Ice Cap aides.

I am just another messenger; remember, "Man's Best Friend". It is truly up to you. I'm not just talking some fundraiser held in the suburbs where you serve Chardonnay and you think that you're politically active. I mean you get out there, roll up your sleeves, in the mud, in your face, and fight for your life politics! Do you need help from the Irish Setters and Wolfhounds? Your future does depend upon the outcome. That is if you want your subjective version of reality to manifest on earth. If not your world may become a real totalitarian corporate nightmare if you're an American, if you live in Canada, the Great White North, plan on continuing to be a satellite puppet for a bad regime. Enough of the fire and brimstone, history will back me up on this. You just get out there and start swinging from your gut, and I'll watch the house, and do my guard dog thing. Relax and remember the universe is a perfect organism, I'll play my part and you play yours. Oh, by the way, if you see ex President Nixon's dog, don't trust him, he's one tricky dick.

Good luck and God speed (I'm not to sure what that really means. It sounds cool and creepy both at the same time). Now go, go do, to do is to be, to be is to do. Quit reading and go do. An dally an dally!

Daisy (D): Wilson what are you doing?

Wilson (W): I'm right in the middle of what I think May just be some of my best work.

D: It's time for dinner.

W: Don't bother me I don't want to loose my train of thought. I feel the muse is striking and the words are flowing right through me.

D: Flowing through whom?

W: Through me!

D: What?

W: Don't interrupt me right now.

D: What?

W: I said, oh forget it, the muse has passed. How many times have I told you to not call me when I'm writing?

D: It's dinnertime though and I know you haven't eaten in awhile and your blood sugar must be getting low. Go wash up and come to the table, the kids should be here any minute. Come on honey wash up and then come help me set the table.

W: Ok, I must be getting hungry; I was thinking of luncheon meats and just realized that I spelled the Dalai Lama's name wrong.

D: Well he is compassion incarnate; I think his Holiness will let you slide.

Flock of Seagulls

You humans make us canines laugh, sadness is more the appropriate emotion. What I'm talking about is the outcome of all your advanced technology in effect has caused indirectly or directly our planets demise. You as a species have polluted the land and water with toxic chemicals not to mention the deteriorating ozone layer from floral carbons and green house gases. You guys are slick. Were all these catastrophes random accidents or was someone in charge and you followed them like lemmings into the sea?

Don't bother answering, my question was rhetorical. The answers obvious, you're a bunch of morons. No actually idiots wrapped inside the body of morons. It escapes me how the infinite universe in all its wisdom and creative intelligence gave you the opposable thumbs and to think that you made weapons of mass destruction with them. Incredible.

Imagine if the birds had the opposable thumbs by now? This is a species that are totally telepathic and move as one mind. Have you ever seen a flock of seagulls? No, not the rock band! How about 1,000 sparrows moving as one? It's the creative universal mind of God just showing you what's out there, just giving you a taste, a hint at the infinite possibilities. But no, your genetic strain came from monkeys, ooh ooh ooh ahh ahh ahh ee ee ee. Oh you're a real class act monkey man. You definitely need to be hanging out with the

Flock of Seagulls

"Seeing Eye" dogs. The "Eyes" are a teaching sect of canines that have attained illumination and enlightenment. If your not at the level to where you can communicate to all species and vegetation telepathically then you'll have to hang out with the seeing eye dogs.

The one or two of you that does rise above the pack, instead of trying to show the others and start to move as one like the sparrows, you actually turn on each other. Manipulate, oppress and bomb each other. The ones that have risen to power inebriate the rest through alcohol and drugs and keep them entertained through sports. Imagine how distracted, manipulated and numbed a mind has to be to think a sports score is more important than the emanate destruction of a planet? Well maybe if you have a wager on the game, that's another matter. Anyway, you ever wonder why the dogs crap on your lawn, its called contempt, distain.

You humans are pathetic. You don't know Jack Squat! I'll prove it. Jack could you please come in here for a minute?

Jack (J):	I'm smoking a cigar.
Wilson (W):	That's ok, Bonnie will just think Todd's been smoking and he'll catch hell; just come in for a moment.
J:	You know we're late for the poker game?
W:	I know, this will just take a minute.
J:	I'm in, what's up?
W:	Jack take a look out there, do you recognize anybody?
J:	No.

W: I rest my case. Thanks Jack I'll meet you in the car. Lets take the 350 Grayhound powered engine out tonight. They finally perfected the steering and peddle mechanisms. By the way, check if there's a cannoli missing from the box?

                                                  Wilson

Letter from Todd

I am sending you and a few other friends this letter, because I feel my dog Wilson has been writing to you. His behavior has been strange recently. Wilson has been going to my bank disguised as me and has been cashing my checks. The only way I found out was that there is $3,000.00 worth of doggie toys in his room. Wilson has been hanging out with Steve Martin's dog who I feel is a bad influence on him, Daisy says that's just an excuse and I am in denial.

The only other explanation I have is that Wilson and Daisy were at a cocktail party at Fred and Wilma's where Wilson ate a bad pickled doe doe egg. The clinical diagnosis is called dippy do dalitas.

I'm thinking of sending Wilson to Vice President (the evil torturous de facto President, you didn't think big business would actually entrust a grade C average monkey to protect their polluting economic interests and run the country did you?) Dick Chaney's behavioral modification and re-indoctrination summer camp. They offer skeet-shooting, quail hunting, first aid, facial reconstructive surgery, law skirting and other outdoor recreational wholesome activities.

So until Wilson starts acting like everybody else, "normal", gets in line with the status quo, stop making waves, I implore you, please do not write him back, that will only encourage him.

Sincerely,
Todd

Hot Body

Lee,

I hear your brother wrote you and tried to convince you not to write me, never mind that, he was only kidding, you and Susan can write. I have to be careful though; he won't let me on the typewriter. Daisies running interference now for me by having a discourse with Todd about atomic accelerators and the mistakes Stephen Hawking made. It's fun to watch Todd's eyes glaze over when Daisy really starts to turn up the heat by quoting Quantified research.

I'm writing to tell you what a laugh Daisy and I had about the letter Todd wrote to Susan to pick up her spirit a few months ago. It was hilarious, Daisy laughed so hard when she was drinking, water came out of her nose. Every time he walks by we snicker behind his back.

He probably meant well in his own twisted kind of way: Susan not feeling well, having to go to the doctors, wondering if she had cancer or be disfigured. I'm glad everything is fine now, but can you imagine telling one's sister-in-law "don't worry you still have a Hot Body" to pick up her spirits?

After all the psychology books he has read I could imagine him saying something boring like "I have unconditional positive regard for you", get well. Maybe even take a step up and quote-international movie stars like George Hamilton or George Clooney by saying "you are a timeless beauty" rest and get well.

Those are all still socially acceptable, but a "hot body"? Come on now, that's something a ragged syphilitic hobo Ranting about socialism outside a deli would say. That moron can't even send a generic valentine card now without you being on him like white on rice.

Daisy and I understand that you have to kill him. Say no more, you have to do what you have to do. The Bible never makes reference to Cain after he slain his brother Able. The real historical fact is that Cain led a quiet, pleasant life afterwards. Listen you need to raise the bar high and make a strong statement, set an example to any future would be leering relatives. This is a matter of family honor.

I think he's kind of expecting it to. He's a little worried that when he comes down to Florida to visit, you're going to pull a "Fredo" on him. You know, have him whacked when he's out fishing with his Grand-nephew Sam.

What you really need to do is to lull him into a false sense of security. Take him out to dinner, a restaurant like Santasiero's, where he'll feel relaxed and comfortable. In the bathroom, there still is an old fashion pull-handle toilet where you could hide a piece behind the top tank. Then come out blasting. Just make sure it's a loud cannon, to scare off any nosey, busybody bystanders. Walk quickly, but don't run. Do not stare anyone in the eyes directly, don't look away either, just let your piece slide down from your hand. You better wear a glove that you can ditch later.

Have a good get away driver ready. I suggest using Carl, he's cool under fire and no one would suspect. Don't use Maria's Frank; guys named Frank get implicated too easily. For example: Frankie six fingers, Frankie the knife, Frankie mad dog. You see where I'm going with this? It only brings on the heat. Now a name like Carl on the other hand brings images of Lederhosen, sausage and beer. You just can't help but like a guy named Carl, remember the Yaz from the Boston Red Sox? Listen, just don't make me sub-contract this out to the Doberman Pincers, they're one psychotic bunch.

Good luck,
Wilson

Remorse

Lee,

Listen, Daisy and I have been rethinking this whole whacking Todd business now that Todd is letting me use the typewriter again. With Todd gone we realize that we'll have no one to support us in the lifestyle we've become accustomed to, which does include doggie treats. Besides you don't want us moving in with you and Susan. Daisy's breath, well let's just say it is not the sweetest. I fart a lot plus mark my territory, which is no exact science. It's very subjective. If you have a Casmir coat, I just may find it threatening … gone … you know what I mean?

Come on really, to say Susan is beautiful is like saying the sky is blue, the birds have wings, Todd's just pointing out the obvious. It really is self-evident.

So we feel you should let sleeping dogs lie (no pun intended).

Come on. Forget about it,
Wilson

Our Afghan Sisters

Daisy (D): I have been thinking about the Afghan female canines in Afghanistan. We need to be in solidarity with them, support their fight. The male canines consider them second-class citizens. Can you imagine having to walk behind your mate and keep your face covered with a veil? My Wilson would never do that to me, would you Wilson? Wake up Wilson. Wilson!

Wilson (W): What's up sugar lips?

D: Stop that, I know you've been watching me type. So why is it?

W: It's because the males don't want other males checking out their bitches.

D: Sounds a bit immature doesn't it?

W: Sure does honey bun.

D: Knock it off. This is serious. It appears that all the males do is screw the females and have them cook, clean, and take care of the children. All while they relax, do business and smoke the hookah.

W: Am I supposed to say something? You're giving me that look. Ok, how about that the females are not allowed to vote, didn't bite their husbands, and or didn't see each other as one spiritual unit emanating from God. Pick one.

D: How about that the males indoctrinated them into a belief system that forever keeps them enslaved as second-class citizens? The males figured that if they make up a set of rules and laws decreed from a made up higher power, like Ali or God, they just might pull the wool over the female's eyes.

W: I think they have, it's called a veil.

D: I think that's just awful. Are they in the dark ages? They're worse than T.V. preachers. They won't take your life savings, but they'll throw you in jail or kill you. Is there anything lower than someone using religion to advance his or her political agenda?

W: No poochie cakes. They are real Neanderthal scumbags.

D: Stop that.

W: Yes dear.

D: Wilson, this is serious. Why don't you, the Mastiffs, and Rottweilers go over there and crack some skulls?

W: Violence begets violence. How about educating the Afghani females?

D: That will take too long, sometime you can nudge someone gently to change. In this case their maladaptive belief system is so ingrained, you'll need a baseball bat.

W: You do know that these dogs are so out of touch with reality if you tell them that they're full of crap, a mindless unquestioning cretin, a delusional dogmatic fool who is afraid to stand up and do the right thing which is equality for the sexes. They'll probably politely tell you "that is your own particular belief system" and then kill you. You do remember that these dogs are crazy? They believe that when they die they'll go to a place called heaven and 72 virgins will be waiting for them. Imagine a religion that promises some hot action in the after life if you go out and kill today? That is one smart nasty political machine. Daisy, my lovie dove honey pie. Dogs, like the human species, also evolve at different rates, understand?

D: I understand, you better not be calling me lovie dove honey pie.

Saint Patty's Day

I want to thank you for your thoughtfulness in sending me that humorous cartoon of the dog telling his owner how much he hates him. That is exactly how I feel about my owner. For example, last week was Saint Patrick's Day. By the way, us canines say Saint Patty's Day, being that Saint Patrick's dog was a tall Irish Wolfhound named Patty, and the celebration is really in her honor. Wow, what a looker too, long legs, a big set of … teeth. Anyway, Daisy and I hosted a Saint Patty's day party in our home when the family was out. We had a few friends over including the Fitzpatrick's and Fahey's, Irish setters and the Garrigan's and Mal-oney's, Irish Wolfhounds, all couples are from out of town. Daisy even painted her nails green for the occasion.

Well we're all having a good time, but after a few pints of green beer, it's time to relieve ones bladder. As a proper host I'm not going to ask my guests to go outside in the cold and snow, so I thought ahead. Todd has this nice soft green floor mat in his tool room right next to his toolbox, plus the room is heated too. I ask you, what says welcome friends come urinate more than a green mat in a heated private room? Especially when the urine soaked rugs vapors come quaffing up. The aromas like a bouquet on a rare Cabernet, full but not to heady.

Saint Patty's Day 65

To make a long story short Todd and Bonnie come home early, unexpected and shut down the party. I spent the rest of the evening outside chained on a leash, tied to a pole once again by the human mind. You know, this is starting to get old, fast. How degrading? Not to mention the humiliation of having our guests leave early, especially when the ladies made ordure's.

Then, Todd lights into me about my behavioral problems. First off, I don't buy into nor accept his viewing lens of me, via Psychology, as being a legitimate science. Psychology is more like a new linguistic Fascism to control and manipulate the ignorant masses. Secondly, I realize my infinite compassion and patience is finite and it is getting thin, real thin. I may even bite the S.O.B.

Thankfully I remember the great gurus, shaman, and teachers of my past, like "Crow Dog", "Lama Dog Gone It" and "Guru Dog Day", but he only taught in the afternoon. I would also be remiss if I didn't mention "Shaman Dog Days Of", but again he only taught in the summer. They all professed non-violent consciousness expansion and transformation of cell tissue rather than violence.

I have to go now and give Todd some of Daisy's kibble.

Peace,
Wilson

Pipe and Slippers

Get a load of this. The other day Todd's walking around in the middle of the afternoon with his silk pajamas on and he tells me to go fetch him his pipe and slippers. Can you believe the audacity? So I tell him quit being delusional. Who the hell does he think he is to be ordering me around? I understand my duties are guarding the house, that's self-evident being that I'm the one with teeth. A pipe and slippers, no freaking way! Is he the king of Siam? I even hear his dog doesn't do that. Besides, Todd doesn't even smoke a pipe, that crazy coot.

He never ceases to amaze me. I think he's lost in some Hugh Hefnerian fantasy, pipe and slippers my ass! What's next a sex grotto?

If you think this is the part of my story where I pontificate some message to humanity, where the soccer moms, the factory workers and the current new age counter culture all unite as one glorious harmonic for a hopeful tomorrow, well maybe in December 2012, but not today.

What I will say though is bite me! You rag tag bag of misfits. Where were you when the powers that be crushed the future of the electric car (100 mph, 120miles between recharges, this is common sense!) or Universal Health Care ten years ago? (Tax dollars used for health instead of financing war for the military industrial complex). If you don't start a peaceful revolution or at least throw those pompous windbags out of office that you were manipulated to elect, you will continue to be indoctrinated, living a lie, clouded by your own state of darkness. Hopefully you will be a better person than your elected U.S. Congressman. These are the weasels that sellout the country's greater good to corporate lobbyists on a daily basis to line their own pockets with gold. You can smell their souls rotting from here. The mindless wretched refuse of society in suit and tie no less. Is it at this point those humans lose their humanity by selling each other out to suffer because of greed? My compassion for their ignorance and utter mindlessness is that I don't slice them in two. I can't, I don't have thumbs to hold my samurai sword (a symbolic gift given by Master Tatsuo Shimabuku 10th Don). Dogs would never do this to each other, well other than Pit Bulls but humans taught them the selfish behavior of "I" instead of "US", as in U.S.A.

When your mind finally clears from all the years of propaganda, indoctrination and from the stress of your American lifestyle forced upon you by the few who run the country, you will know these words to be true. Only then will the many take their shackles of fear off, know that they are not alone, stiffen their backbone and begin to take back the country from the greedy few. Come on, you're Americans not Americants. Remember the French, every couple of hundred years they lob the heads off the ruling class just to keep them honest. Don't you just love those Frenchies and their Poodles. Remember that they did give us the Statue of Liberty! Remember liberty?

Change your thoughts and you change the world. Ok, I'll start you off, love each other, be kind to each other, take care of each other and our planet like you were going to be here for a thousand years, get active, lobby door to door, talk to your neighbor and vote. In the words of an old IBM logo: THINK.

Peace,
Wilson

Doggie Style

Wilson (W): Daisy, what was that one sexual position called that when you do it correctly you attain enlightenment, but if done incorrectly you sever your spine?

Daisy (D): It's called the "Nirvana Crusher". Why, what are you up to now?

W: I'm writing a book on doggie porn. I think the pornography publishers are the only ones left that might publish our work.

D: What?

W: I figured after that piece you wrote on the repression of Afghanistan females, no mainstream publisher would pick us up, to controversial, a real political hot potato.

D: Yea your right, not to mention you wrote that the Great Danes should molest the President for crimes against humanity, fronting for big business interests in other countries. The C.I.A., F.B.I., N.S.C. and the I.R.S will be looking into and auditing us

	for years to come. Also, think of the violent letters from the Fundamentalist faction of the American Kennel Club.
W:	Yes, you're right, but I didn't say which President. If asked it was President Taft. Ok?
D:	When the unemployed World War I Veterans peacefully marched on Washington, D.C., they drew gunfire from their own Government. Do you think that will happen to us?
W:	Worse, were not even Veterans.
D:	Do you think that the Government will put us in an internment camp like they did to110,000 United States citizens of Japanese descent when World War II broke out?
W:	That's a given for sure.
D:	How about those American backed death squads from Central America they used in the 1980's to squelch the people's democratic movement?
W:	Possibly. They did rape and kill Catholic nuns you know, big business doesn't fool around!
D:	I see a pattern here, of government/business oppression against its own people. Why don't humans do something?
W:	They forget, as Gore Vidal would say, it's the "United States of Amnesia". They keep humans occupied with mortgages to pay, school loans, heating and electric bills, bake good sales, who has the time? Not to mention

distracting us with shiny sparkly things. Ah, sweet, sweet shiny sparkly things.

D: Wilson, snap out of it!

W: Sorry.

D: Do you think the Government will burn us to the ground, like they did the Symbionese Liberation Army in 1974? Wilson I saw them die right on TV, definitely a strong message to its citizens to not be messing around with the grandchildren of billionaires and the banking system.

W: Daisy your parents weren't newspaper tycoons by any chance?

D: No, they were poor, just every day people.

W: Then the government won't care about us. We'll probably just be arrested and forced to watch sit-coms on television to lull us into a state of complacency. It'll be like getting a lobotomy.

D: Well at least we won't have to hang out with Todd anymore.

W: Yes, this does have an upside; we won't have to listen to his incessant ranting that the only great rock bands were from 1967 to 1972. If I have to listen to The Cream's drummer play "Toad" (a 20 minute drum solo) one more time my head is going to explode!

D: Well, Ginger Baker is one of the greatest drummers ever!

W: Yes I agree, but does he have to play the solo non-stop!

D: I'm going to miss being with Beth and Aric; they're so kind and fun to be around. Not to mention Bonnie's cooking and the walks she took us on.

W: Oh yes Bonnie, sweet, sweet Bonnie.

D: Wilson, knock it off!

W: Hey. I'm just saying.

D: Yes, I know, you just cut that out.

W: Yes dear.

D: I know, let's move to Canada, or to the nearest church and claim sanctuary.

W: It's not the good old days when Prime Minister Pierre Trudeau was hanging out with musicians. Now moving to Canada will buy us just a little time; Canada is slowly becoming a U. S. puppet state, for a bad regime, now that Stephen Harper is Prime Minister.

D: More like Prime Rib.

W: Come on now, lets not sink to those depths of demonizing and name-calling.

D: You're right; I don't know what got into me? It was the thought of having to miss the family and having to eat jail food.

W: I know, why don't we just start practicing all these new positions that I've been reading about in the Kama Sutra and Tantra Yoga books We'll work on them seven days a week, twenty-four hours a day.

D: Knock it off mister!

W: Seriously, I'll write about our experience, we'll make money; it will pay for all our legal fees to fight our incarceration. What do you say; shall I get the jiffy lube?

D: Settle down their Sparky, Bonnie, Todd and the children are still home. Wilson my dear you never cease to amaze me.

W: I'm just saying it's a beautiful night, full moon and I have a new batch of Rudy Valley and Moby Grape records. Who loves you baby?

D: Wilson, your middle initial T definitely stands for trouble.

Doggie Style

Breaking Thin Ice-The Gift

Wilson (W): Daisy, the other day Todd and I were talking and he told me that when he was around seven years old, both he and his older brother Lee fell through the ice out on Lake Erie and survived. Talk about being lucky.

Daisy (D): Wilson when you go to the store could you please play Lucky 7 Lotto today.

W: Seriously, this was an incredible true story to hear. The boys were standing next to each other when they broke thru the ice, both submerged. Todd recalled looking up thru the water and seeing the ice above his head. He grabbed on to his brothers back as they resurfaced to the top of the ice, his brother saying hold on tight.

D: What happened next?

W: Todd watched his brother continually try to climb up on the ice as it continued to break off.

D: Was Todd scared?

W: That's just it he wasn't, not a bit because he was with his older brother.

D: It sure is great to have a big brother that won't let you down.

W: Yes, too bad ours were sold after our mothers had litters.

D: Tell me about it.

W: Eventually his brother was able to slowly edge his shoulder up onto the ice and pull them both up to safety.

D: Incredible!

W: Yes, it turns out that Todd didn't know that his big brother felt bad that he almost got Todd killed. His brother didn't know that Todd on the other hand took his own responsibility for standing to close to his big brother, possibly causing the ice to break and was totally thankful to his big brother for saving his life.

D: Amazing! Extraordinary!

W: Then Todd goes on how every thing that's happened to him since is really a gift, being that he didn't die. All his adventures, his friends, karate, music, his wife, the children, all is a gift. It's funny how two different perspectives come out of one event.

D: Yes, ones perception of reality can be likened to looking into a multi-dimensional gazing crystal, coupled with the realization that everything that happens to you is a manifestation of your own state of consciousness.

W: You've been into your special kibble again haven't you?

D: Yes, can you tell, is it obvious?

W: Da!

D: So what are your points Wilson, that this story reflects, "It's a Wonderful Life", "The Glass Menagerie", cosmic fate, intergalactic destiny, and good fortune? What?

W: No none of that, Its' just good to have a big brother, you never know when he'll come in handy.

The Dog Show

Daisy (D): Wilson honey, what do you want to do today?

Wilson (W): I was thinking that you might want to go to the park with me and see if we could get in on a game of Frisbee, maybe chase a couple of squirrels for fun.

D: There's a dog show in town today and the family is going. I thought we could catch a ride with them.

W: I knew you had something planned, as soon as you say honey, I know it's just a matter of time before I'm hoodwinked into one of your evil plans.

D: Oh stop that. Come on it'll be fun.

W: I don't know, the arena smells of hairspray, some canines are crying because they don't want to be there, it's surreal.

D: So is everything if you look at it that way. It's a matter of perspective and besides that's only a few cases. Most of the dogs

	enjoy being there. Think of it, it's a time for them to socialize and strut their stuff.
W:	Haven't we moved beyond that tawdry sort of thing?
D:	We haven't been out in awhile; we may even run into some old friends. I know how much that means to you. Come on, as I previously mentioned, it'll be fun. We have to hurry if you want to catch a ride with the family. Before we leave, change that awful shirt, who do you think you are Tom Selleck?
W:	It's my favorite shirt, I'm in the zone when I have this shirt on.
D:	I know, but that shirt will set off security alarms at the arena, go change.
W:	Ok, but first we have to go down to the boathouse. There's a dead fish that washed ashore that we could roll around in and have a nice fragrant scent on us before we hop in the car.
D:	Sounds like a plan.

The Dog Show   79

Hero Worship

You know, it seems like forever mankind has always searched to put meaning to life and to their existence. The nuance, metaphor and analogies vary from culture to culture; some use the medium of dance, while others have oral traditions that are passed on through generations. Whatever medium, it's usually an attempt to explain how in the world they arrived and what their relationship to the Universe is. Humans' believing that they did not create the Universe usually attribute creation to some outer force, a higher power that is greater, and then offerings of homage ensue. Maybe all our cognitive wiring is off and we have more of a hand in this than we know? It's always man though who intercedes, a couple of big wigs that are the intermediary between the creator and the rest. Of course there are a bunch of laws that come along with these revelations to manipulate the culture into acting a certain sort of way, like crowd control.

Now in canine ancient mythology we used to worship a large vibrating egg. Eventually we as a species transcended that belief system, to where now we worship nothing. We just believe in the here and now, no past, or future, just the ever present eternal now. This we find meaningful. Don't misunderstand me were definitely kind, respectful and thankful to everything, though the humans never really understood us nor accepted our indigenous way of life.

First they give us blankets infected with small pox disease (like they did to Native American Indians), then they tried to demonize us by giving us the name "Dog", before we as a species used to refer to each other as "Freddie Baby". A typical conversation would go something like this: Hey Freddie Baby how the hell are you? Hey Freddie Baby what's new with you? You get the drift? Then the humans started to domesticate us. Well what can I say; we all went downhill from there as you can surmise by the plastic squeaky toy dangling from my mouth. That reminds me, do you want to play catch after? You see how beaten down we have become? We used to be fearless warriors, and that was just the female of our species!

So now, the Corporate World has taken Mankind to even more hideous depths of deep heinousness. Instead of having humans worshipping the Sun, Zeus, Mohamed, Jesus or a myriad of other characters sent down from central casting, they now have them worshiping Corporate Logos: the new Gods of industry.

I'm starting to believe us canines shouldn't be the ones called: Dog.

Wilson

The A List

Wilson (W): Daisy, let's go visit Stu Got and his family.

Daisy (D): I don't think were really welcomed over the Gots anymore. Ever since you slapped the Mrs. behind, told her to lighten up and quit being so uptight. Plus it didn't help matters when you planted a wet one on her; you know how upset the feminists are about invading personal space. I'm surprised that she didn't knee you in the groin?

W: She did, why do you think I walk with a limp. Well, you calling Stu a crypto fascist puppet for the industrial elite surely did not help matters either. Face it were no longer on the A list, we never were. We were used as fillers for empty space really. We're freaks; you have nine nipples and I have the googel eyes.

D: I still feel you need to read more Emily Post.

W: Sweet, sweet Emily.

D:	Wilson!
W:	Sorry. Does it really matter though that there are no more cocktail parties to go to?
D:	It does give people an opportunity to socialize in a relaxed setting. Not every one can feel comfortable sitting around in a circle chanting.
W:	I realize that, but at cocktail parties there are to many superficial personas. Granted at times I like the conversation light and airy, though with sincerity.
D:	Sounds like a Chant to me. Light and airy with sincerity, light and airy with sincerity. You're just not talking to the right people Wilson, maybe you're the odd ball attracting them?
W:	Do you mind, let's not even go there.
D:	Oh, in denial huh?
W:	You've been into Todd's library reading his books haven't you? Damn those Psychology books.
D:	I have a whole new regime plotted out for you Mister. First, you're going to Behavioral modification class. Then some Cognitive restructuring topped off with Motivational therapy. When's the last time you muscled a little Girl Scout out of her cookies when she came to the door? Maybe some carrot juice might even help you. Anyway though,

	they'll be no more lounging around smoking cigars, listening to Brazilian Samba music for you, not to mention the champagne cocktails!
W:	Daisy, where was that Doberman Pincer's phone number I had?
D:	It was over on the dresser next to your plastic squeaky toy, why do you ask?
W:	No particular reason, nothing special, I just want the Dobermans to pay a visit to Todd.
D:	Aren't the Dobermans kind of violent and psychotic?
W:	No, no not these ones, they're just going to have a nice pleasant talk with Todd about a last straw.

Generation of The Doomed

Daisy (D): Wilson, do you think that the younger generation has their head on straight?

Wilson (W): Of course not, that's why they call it the folly of youth. They're so busy discovering their own sense of self, by the time they wake up to the politics of oppression, they are already owned by the man.

D: What's this man stuff?

W: Haven't you been listening, what are you stupid or something?

D: Hey, hey, hey, knock that off, and to think that I share my water bowl with you.

W: Sorry, I get a little worked up, about the few oppressing the many. The man is a metaphor for any controlling entity that manipulates you and has power over you, in this case I was referring to multi billion dollar multi international corporations that use our own government against its citizens.

D: Oh do go on.

W: You know I love it when you fan my fires of insurrection. Like I was alluding to, by the time our youth have woken up from years of indoctrination, programming and propaganda, they still won't be able to shake free of the controls put in place for them. Haven't you seen the movie Sleeper? Where the hell have you been the past thirty years?

D: Wilson, you're doing that condescending thing that you do so well, again.

W: Sorry, really I'm sorry, I get too worked up. Think about it though, peoples credit cards, phone records, cable bills, the Government knows what you spend, who you speak with, what you watch. Plus you're a walking demographic for the companies that lobbied for this legislation to make money off of your behavioral patterns.

D: At least the Government can't take our stuff and force us into a boat and bring us to another country like they did in past centuries.

W: Sure they can, they're called the IRS and the Customs and Immigration Authority.

D: So what you're implying, with all these eroded civil rights and new government controls in place that our youth are the new generation of the doomed?

W: Wow, I'm impressed, what have you been reading Dostoyevsky, Chomsky, Groucho

& Karl Marx, Martha Mitchell, Hunter Thompson, William Burroughs, South Park, Socrates, The Sex Pistols? What?

D: I get around.

W: Do you see any hope?

D: Yes of course. The youth need to keep voting and stay involved. They're smart; I have high hopes for them.

W: The political machine only picks mundane issues with little relevance to the bigger picture, which is the balance of power. I'm saying the topics of discussion are already limited by the time they're brought to the table.

D: Oh yea, I agree that whoever is in power controls the forum, that's why they're in power, their ruthless. They just give you the illusion that it's a free and open forum.

W: So we're all squared away on the topic for today?

D: Yes, just so long as the youth of today keep voting and remain civically active.

W: Good lets go have lunch, what's on the menu for today?

D: What else, kibble, same as it always was, same as it always was.

W: What I'd give for a pastrami on rye right about now. So Daisy how come we never vote?

D: We are not allowed in the electoral process.

W: What about all the work our forefathers did with the Suffer Jets? I thought we were aligned in helping women achieve the right to vote from the man?

D: We were, the German Shepherds ran security for the women's movement.

W: You mean all the dog doo they back kicked and flung at the riot police during those women's right to vote rallies was all for not.

D: No, it was a victory, women won the right to vote.

W: Politics and administration policies haven't changed much. The man is still in charge or should I say the wo-man?

D: Rome wasn't built in a day, be patient and steadfast to your internal beliefs.

W: I still want the right to vote, but if I bite a Government Official one more time they're going to put me to sleep. At least I want the right to still back kick and fling the doo.

D: Quit being infantile; let's go have lunch.

W: I don't know now, lunch and doo within one sentence of each other is a real turn off. What are you some kind of kook weirdo? You sick-o you.

D: That's it, I'm done, I've had all I can take from you today Mr. T.

Wilson stung by bee

Instant Karma

Wilson (W): Daisy, come quick. Hurry!

Daisy (D): Holy Ba Jesus you look like the Elephant Man, or a disgruntled postal employee. Did a bee sting you, Cujo?

W: It was awful, hideous; it had the body of a crab with two heads, one of an insurance salesman, the other a social worker.

D: Stop goofing around.

W: Yes, it was a bee! Remember you told me to take time and smell the roses, well I was out in the garden just sniffing around and then **BANG!**

D: I was speaking metaphorically. It looks painful.

W: It is, like going to the veterinarian painful.

D: You look like a tick that's ready to pop. You should go to the veterinarian.

W: No way, please just go bring me an antihistamine.

D: Wilson, remember the time you stayed with Crow Dog, the Sioux medicine man, on the Rosebud reservation and Eagle Feather told you that you could tell who's supposed to be at a sacred ceremony, by who's at the sacred ceremony.

W: Yeah so.

D: He was implying that there are no accidents, only what appear to be circumstances.

W: Your point is?

D: That bee sting you received was no accident! Just like yesterday, when the Dobermans for some unknown reason ripped up Todd, they actually rang the doorbell to. The Universe is giving you a message to wake up Wilson, maybe slow down and take a look at how

	you've been moving around in time and space. Also what thoughts that have been running through your head, take a look at those. Maybe help out around the house a little more, rake some leaves, and give me more foot massages.
W:	Settle down there. Your viewpoint is just your subjective interpretation of your perception of the phenomenal world.
D:	You better smarten up Mister and stop quoting Todd. It's so un-you.
W:	You don't think that your particular belief system works in today's business oriented consumer driven society, do you?
D:	It works for me, besides one can be indoctrinated unconsciously to buy and consume and still not bump into bees. Haven't you learned anything, it's you that has to tune in your reception/perception to what the Earth and Universe are telling you.
W:	As I mentioned, your viewpoint is … oh forget it, this conversation is becoming redundant, besides I'm drowsy from the antihistamines.
D:	Wake up Wilson: Instant karma is going to get you, slap you upside your head, better get yourself together darling, pretty soon you're going to be dead.
W:	Please stop singing and pass me the ice pack.

D: I'm just saying: Slow down you're moving to fast, you got to make the morning last…

W: Stop singing! You always have to have the last word!

D: Not really.

Epilogue

Daisy (D): Well Quasi-Motto, you're looking healthier now that the antihistamines have worked. You must be thankful?

Wilson (W): I am continually grateful and thankful to the planet Jupiter's gravitational pull in directing meteors away from Earth and of course the creative intelligence that created this whole ball of wax.

D: So semantically challenged one, is that what you're calling it now a days, a ball of wax? You are so deep and profound, did I forget to mention articulate? What, did you skip metaphysics class that day? Did your car break down, did you bend your tailpipe?

W: Excuse me; the English language is a limited language in these matters. Sanskrit would be more descriptive when discussing spirituality and cosmic dimensions manifesting in the material plane.

D: You don't know Sanskrit do you?

W: No.

D: Did you at least underlay a subliminal message in your letters as you wrote them?

W: Of course, I'm no idiot; the subliminal message was to play more Chuck Berry.

D: You're an idiot, you didn't encourage world peace, share the wealth, stop all war and torture. I'd even settle for stop torturing us with silly dog sweaters, but Chuck Berry?

W: Hey, what can I say; I'm a music lover. What do you think I was doing when you were at the Quilting Circle plotting revolution? I had the tunes cranked and was rocking!

D: Seriously Wilson, do you feel that you helped the humans in any way with your letters? Maybe tapped into the universal collective unconscious, as Carl Jung would say? Maybe even unlock a fragment of their psyche enabling epiphanies to unfold? How about triggering a genetic compound that's been lying dormant, just waiting?

W: Possibly. Though we did commit the seven deadly sins while trying to awaken the masses.

D: You have to break a couple of eggs if you want to make an omelet you know. What about Quantum Theory and Heidelberg's uncertainty principal? Considering the current state that humanity is in as the "position" coupled with your thoughts

Epilogue

as the "momentum", there's a probability that your observations could influence humanities outcome.

W: I'm uncertain about that uncertainty, and probably not for that probability.

D: Well Wilson, what are you going to do next?

W: I'm going to have a cannoli, could you please pass me the box? Dam, there's one missing.

D: Wait, there's a note at the bottom of the box.

W: Who's it from?

D: It's from Todd and it's in "Klingon".

W: What an A-hole. What's it say?

D: It says, "My Philosopher buddy Seneca ate the Cannoli, deal with it!"

W: Figures. Hey Daisy, by the way, when did you ever learn "Klingon"?

D: Like I was saying, I get around.

Post Epilogue—
I Found Jimmy Hoffa

Daisy (D): Wilson, what dog in their right mind writes a post epilogue in a book? Not to mention a page that's numbered 22.5, you were just too lazy to redo this chapter weren't you?

Wilson (W): Does it matter? Who's going to buy the book anyway? Anarchists don't have any money, they're always on the run, there's no stable life, ergo: no dogs around. So who really is my demographic? Rich anarchists with dogs, they're called Capitalists! Lets go take a walk outside to self reflect and ponder on what our next move will be.

D: I know, lets dig up the soup bone you buried a month ago; it should be just about ready.

W: I'm not too sure I remember where I buried the bone, my memory is not what it used to be since I turned five.

D: Tell me about it, were both past middle age.

Post Epilogue—I Found Jimmy Hoffa

W: I think I found it, no those are just Todd's car keys I buried one year ago.

D: Don't you think you should give them back?

W: No, let him sweat it out a few more days.

D: That's your eighth hole you just dug.

W: I still remember how to count you know! Wait, I've got something.

D: Is it the soup bone?

W: It's a bone, not the soup bone. It's a body!

D: Are you serious?

W: I kid you not. Come help me dig, check if there's some identification around?

D: There's a Teamster I.D. His name says Jimmy Hoffa. Should we call someone?

W: We're in enough trouble as it is, and stop chewing.

D: Well then, let's prop him up so he can scare the squirrels.

W: Could you please show some respect? What we are going to do is, when the Governments henchmen come to take us away and put us in an internment camp for our book, will trade off Todd as the fall guy. Let him take the rap for Hoffa. We'll be off the hook from the Government and think

D: of the favors that will be owed to us by a few powerful unnamable people?

D: You do have a point, no Todd, no jail, and favors owed. It's like having your cake and eating it too.

W: Or killing two birds with one stone.

D: With Jimmy gone, who's going to scare the squirrels out of the backyard?

W: We'll hire the cats. Ever since NAFTA and Globalization, most of the cats' jobs have been outsourced to Third World Countries at cheaper labor costs. There are a lot of cool cats out of work that need money.

D: You're not suggesting we degrade ourselves by conning the cool cats into working for cheap labor?

W: No, we'll hire the cool cats, but at a good wage, everybody deserves respect, and a life style, everybody, everybody.

This Is Not A Fellini Movie

Wilson (W): So, Daisy, I was thinking, do you want to do it?

Daisy (D): Do what?

W: You know, do it!

D: By any chance, are you referring to The Divine Dance, The Sacred Union, and The Cosmic Interplay between souls?

W: What? No, I'm just asking if you want to do it?

D: Well, you're quite the charmer. Listen Wilson, this will never become a children's book talking like that. Wilson, Wilson!

W: I'm thinking about what you said. What I mean by "doing it" was do you want to have some milk and cookies and take a nap?

D: Ok now, that's more like it, I'll play along. Then Wilson maybe after our naptime would you like to play ruff ruff with the chu chu train?

W: Now you really threw me off. Would this train by any chance be going through a tunnel?

D: No you idiot, I'm trying to help you out if you still want this to be a children's book.

W: I'm confused.

D: Listen up slick, if our discussion was a movie it would be directed by Mr. Rogers not Federico Fellini! Understand?

W: Oh yea, I understand, that goes without saying, sure. There's just one thing I don't understand?

D: What's that?

W: Will there be any humping involved?

D: That's it; I'm out of here.

The Dixie Chicks Canines

Daisy (D): I still can't believe what happened to the Dixie Chicks Canines. All the conservative dogs in their neighborhood won't speak to them just because their owners talked poorly of the President.

Wilson (W): They didn't call him a war criminal that should be indicted for crimes against humanity!

D: No.

W: How about a moron going off half-cocked whose macho bravado arrogance is inappropriate in the world arena of politics?

D: No.

W: How about him taking the high ground having wisdom into other cultures, setting the stage for harmony and class equality?

D: Now you're dreaming. No, the girls said that they were embarrassed that the President lived in their state.

W: All that hoopla, just for that? Hell, I've called him worse.

D: Yes Wilson, don't remind me.

W: What's the big deal, so the people who bought their albums in the past won't any more? That demographic is indoctrinated from years of government propaganda not to mention being lulled into complicacy from watching TV sit-coms. What did they expect?

D: Well at least you didn't call them hicks, but they still won't have an audience, they'll become poor, their dogs might starve!

W: Tell them to relax, stiffen their backbone and play music to a more open minded public. Those girls are virtuosos, I'm sure they can retool their chord progressions. Write a letter to the dogs; tell them they can join our Circus act if they would like to support their masters. Also, tell those dogs to tell the girls to stop doing interviews with that old Nixon crony, Diane Sawyer. I'm sure they had their fill of Sawyer's snide smirks and condescending glances. Don't they know that she is just a pretty face the government puts on to front for them? Imagine getting one of the Dixie Chicks to cry on national television, Sawyers' a bully.

D: Wilson you know it's unpatriotic to say anything contrary other than the administration's viewpoint.

W: Patriotism—oh yes, the last refuse of a scoundrel. Us dogs are the real patriots, encouraging the many to vote out the few in office who have screwed up this country, which includes making each citizen suspect of each other. The culture of paranoia: the perfect way to never have the people join together as one and take their country back. Forever to be marginalized out of the political arena, separated, powerless.

D: You just wait until Katie Couric sinks her nails into you; they're going to have a field day demonizing you in the press, maybe even calling you a mongrel dog.

W: Well if the shoe fits. Hey, wait a minute, I'm a pedigree and I can vote!

D: Wilson, you can't vote, remember?

W: Oh brother!

Something/Anything

Daisy (D): I was talking to Sally the Schnauzer who lives down the road and she said that her owner said you have a warped perception of reality.

Wilson (W): Her owner's in denial, she can't accept my version of reality because it threatens her version. She's not ready to accept that everything that she has been taught has been just someone else's version of reality, most of which is not based in truth or fact. It hurts her too much to accept that reality. It's easier for her not to question and just point the finger at me.

D: Well, she says that you're in denial and you're the one that's pointing the finger.

W: That's just it, reality is up for grabs unless you have a real strong hold on what really is truth, how else do you explain 50% of the country voting for Bush other than the median educational level of the Sothern States is 6th grade. It's because they don't know which way is up, or they gave up and accepted someone else's version of truth. What does your gut tell you? It doesn't lie. I bet they never taught you that in grammar school. Remember grammar school? You sat in rows, had to raise your hand. This is where the conditioning to be submissive begins. You are taught that you are not in power, any dialogue contrary to that, you are conditioned to be suspect of. Does Sally know that her owner is afraid of the self-inquiry of who am I, where am I, where am I going and will I be able to break a twenty when I get there? Does she know that her loving, kind and thoughtful owner is also conditioned and can be manipulated?

D: Of course, how else do you explain the air-conditioned doghouse with cable TV that Sally talked her in to installing?

W: Don't you just love Schnauzers, not to mention their bookkeeping and accounting skills?

The Special Kibble

Wilson (W): Daisy, what's up with the special kibble you eat?

Daisy (D): Well, I've noticed it has four stages. The first is the lower material plane. This is where I have to go to the bathroom and excrete all toxins from my body. The second stage is upper material physical plane. That is where I have to stretch because the energy is starting to move through my muscles. The Kundalini is starting to move up my spine. It's like getting unstuck, loosening up. The third stage is more astral/mental in nature. This is where I realize the mistakes I have made with interacting with my fellow species and mankind and of course you, darling. If I do not make amends here in my mind, I will not be allowed to move onto the fourth stage. Once I have made peace I move into pure creative energy. This is the stage where your thoughts manifest in the material plane on a subatomic cellular level. It's also a stage of deep profound insight where you just enjoy being incarnate and appreciative of all the spirit energy and life around you that you are part of. This is quite humbling if you are sensitive enough to be aware that this is a blessed state of consciousness then you and your perspective will be transformed forever. Got all that?

W: Yes, I was checking to see if you knew.

The Special Kibble

The Dinner Table

Daisy (D): Wilson, How long have we been sitting and hoping Todd would give us a scrap of food from the dinner table?

Wilson (W): Too long, do you think that he even notices us? Hey, Stunot, we're over here. Yo, monkey man, how about that piece right there, no not in your mouth, damn! He usually gives us something if we're totally quiet and still. Hey, we're over here!

D: What is he a deaf, dumb and blind kid? Why isn't he paying attention to us?

W: He's mean, but no pinball wizard that's for sure.

D: Why don't we just roll him, take the food and be done with it?

W: No, you know how crazy he gets when his blood sugar is low.

D: What are you doing now?

W: I'm going to burn a hole in his brain with my eyes, give him the googol stare.

D: Oh, that's brilliant, why don't you just bore him to death while you're at it? How about doing one of your cutesy poses?

W: No way, I'm not going to lower and degrade myself, If he can't be sensitive to our needs it's his loss, I'll just go take his wallet and car keys.

D: You don't call that degrading, plus illegal?

W: What court in their right mind would convict us? Come on look at him. They should be paying us to hang out with him.

D: Well, you do have a point. If we do make it out to the restaurant, I want the real surf and turf, not a tuna fish sandwich with beef gravy like you tried to pull last time.

W: Lobster, filet and champagne it is my darling, Todd is paying. Let's just max out the card while we're at it. We'll even send him a thank you basket from the florist.

D: Oh that's good, let's sign the card from Todd, that will really wig him out.

W: Yes, he'll think that he's in some parallel Universe where his double is out having a really wonderful, fantastic and expensive time, but Todd has to pay the bill.

D: We'll watch his mind start to implode upon itself as his brain tries to make sense of the dichotomous parody.

W: Does it get any better than this?

D: Well, yes but I can appreciate your sentiment, lets go eat.

5 minutes later————

D: Wilson, be careful backing out of the driveway, with those eyes. You clipped a bush!

W: Relax.

D: I've been meaning to ask, why did you put the **EPILOGUE** three quarters into the book?

W: The book is like a double album in music. It's two books in one. The second part is random spattering, like a Jackson Pollock painting, but instead it's Abstract Expressionist Writing. I'm breaking the mold, charting new territory.

D: What about all the typographical errors?

W: It's all freedom baby, like a Pollock painting, it's also part of the readers freedom to interpret my spelling and grammatical intention.

D: Sounds like bullshit to me.

W: Yes, like Art or Politics; I need a publisher & spin-doctor with an advertising budget.

D: Oh, brother.

Wilson backing Jaguar out of driveway

The Key

Daisy (D): Wilson, quit chewing on your plastic hotdog and listen to me for a moment. I've been up in the library and I've been reading a few books and I think I'm on to something.

Wilson (W): What are you talking about?

D: I've noticed that when I read books about mystics from different religious sects, it appears that they have all been to the same territory of mind. They all have similar versions of the Universe as being a direct spiritually profound experience, even though they come from different cultures and are centuries apart from each other.

W: So ones interpretation of the phenomenal world is not a totally subjective experience.

D: Yes, I think I am on to something. I started looking at Todd's books and certificates and I started to notice a connection. Did you know that the ten Separath of the Holy Kabbalah and the twenty two Major Arcana

	of the Tarot, which add up to thirty-two match the thirty two degrees of Masonry?
W:	No I didn't know that.
D:	That's just one of many systems up there.
W:	What mystery are you uncovering now Nancy Drew?
D:	It's an esoteric map on how to connect with the creative infinite intelligence of the Universe. Being that there are other dimensions than this one. There is a way to transverse and bring things into this physical dimension and make manifest. Remember the Universe is like a loaf of bread with the slices (dimensions) all lined up in a row.
W:	Come on, you've been into the kibble.
D:	No I haven't, I'm serious. Todd has books that date back centuries. Look at the certificates. One is from a Pope, another from the Knights Templar, another from a President, even a letter from Dionysus herself thanking him for the wild parties. I think I'm on to a giant conspiracy, or some secret society.
W:	Your just being paranoid, and your starting to wig me out.
D:	Think of it, why all the years of Martial Arts training? All the years Todd spent living with Sages and Shaman, not to mention

The Key 115

all this evidence! I've only gotten thru ten books and there is three thousand more in the library. Plus, he hasn't aged a day in ten years.

W: There's probably a portrait of Dorian Gray in the attic!

D: Why would a man actively involved in and of this world now be a total recluse? I think he's getting ready for some big changes.

W: If you tell me spaceships behind the moon, I'll put you out of your misery right here and now!

D: Ok, I admit I did go a little overboard there, letting my imagination run away, but I'm serious Wilson. There are no accidents in the universe, only what appear to be circumstances. It is no accident that we are here, part of this realization at this time.

W: There are a lot of random accidents. I think your mind is seeing what it wants to see so you can explain your world to make sense to and of yourself.

D: That sounds so sweet and politically correct. Why don't you take your own advice and knock it off! I'm on to something here! Maybe we are the genetic descendents of a bloodline Todd's sworn to guard and protect?

W: I think we're the ones who are supposed to do the guarding, and it's of the children and the house! As far as a bloodline: It's called guard dog!

D: Why doesn't he just tell us?

W: Tell us what? I just knew you'd get in some kind of trouble reading his books. I warned you, but noooo, you didn't listen!

D: Eureka, that's it! Pearls before swine (Matthew 7:6), that's why it's a secret.

W: What was this "it" again?

D: Only the ones that can figure out the connections get to partake in the banquette feast, so to speak. Many are called but few are chosen (Matthew 22:14). This is the **Golden Dawn**ing of an **Illuminati**ngly wonderful age.

W: Maybe for some. Have you seen the statistics for the National reading level? This is mostly an illiterate society, and world for that matter. I would liken this time to more of a Dark Age. There is still a lot of war created by stupid humans with bizarre beliefs.

D: Yes Wilson, though life is still a cosmic dance, a miracle to behold, cherish and protect.

W: I agree life is a cosmic dance. Let's bow gracefully to each other in honor of this miraculous dance that we call life, and dance the dance.

D: Dance we shall, and dance we shall!

Wilson in Muumuu dress

J. Edgar Hoover & the Tea Party Girls

Wilson (W): Oooh my aching belly, I need some bicarbonate of soda, I ate too many cookies at the tea party.

Daisy (D): Where in the world have you been and what in the world are you doing in a dress? Who do you think you are J. Edgar Hoover?

W: Its action ware apparel and who's J. Edgar Hoover?

D: He was the Director of the Federal Bureau of Investigation for decades, who was also a homosexual transvestite. He spied and kept records on millions of United States citizens and Presidents just to keep from being outed himself. He was one twisted soul, especially attacking his own kind. No self-respecting transvestite would be associated with his likes. The Government hides his twisted ness just like the Chinese Government hides the rebellion at Tiananmen Square.

W: Seems like he tried taking the long way around to get his way.

D: The Mob has a photo of J. Edgar in a red chiffon cocktail dress, that's why he always said there was no such thing as organized crime.

W: What does this have to do with me anyways?

D: I think you like wearing a dress.

W: No it's not a dress, its action ware apparel, besides I'm trying to tell you that I was absconded by the Tea Party Girls, dressed up, taken to a tea party and fed tea and crumpets. Oh! I need a Tums.

D: So that's your lame story? Hey, here comes Butchie the Bulldog and Ralphie the Yorkshire terrier.

W: Tell them I'm not home, I don't want them see me in my action ware apparel.

D:	Hey Butchie, Ralphie, come quick, Wilson's in a dress, he thinks he's J. Edgar Hoover.
W:	Good grief! Would someone pass me a Rolaids?
Butchie (B):	Did the Tea Party Girls get Wilson?
D:	WHAT!! They actually exist?
B:	Yea, they are a group of old 10 year old girls that dress up the animals in the neighborhood, serve tea and crumpets and teach proper etiquette, manners and civility. They put bonnets and white gloves on Ralphie and me. We didn't mind, they were very polite and kind.

Those girls displace such a powerful vibration of courtesy and manners that can be felt for miles around. They are one powerful force to be reckoned with. Nobody messes with the Tea Party Girls. Not even Bloods, Crypts, Latin Kings, not even the Hells Angels. It's a beautiful thing to watch, gang members saying: yes mam, no mam, please and thank you, holding doors open for the elderly. When a group of irate 10 year old girls start wielding purses stuffed with gummy bears that hit you with the force of Thor's Hammer, being that you did not lift your pinky finger while sipping tea; that will put the fear of God in you, let me tell you!

	They even taught Ralphie to not lick himself in public.
D:	Why are you still doing that Ralphie?
Ralphie (R):	Well for starters: because I can!
D:	You just cut that out mister, the ladies don't think you're very funny at all! Why haven't I been invited to a Tea Party?
B:	You're scheduled next week Daisy for their symposium on halitosis and dental hygiene.
D:	Are the Tea Party Girls famous?
B:	Let's just say above Emily Post's fireplace mantle, is a picture of the Tea Party Girls.
W:	Daisy, ask them why they're here and please bring me an Alka-Seltzer.
D:	Wilson's wondering why
B:	Yea I heard, its bulk trash next Tuesday and we're wondering if you want to tip over a couple of garbage cans with us.
W:	Yes, if I'm feeling better.
B:	Wilson, the key to life is moderation. Next time don't eat so many sugar cookies.
W:	The Tea Party Girls taught me the art of moderation thru the enlightened path of excess. Boy what a lesson!

D: Wilson, by any chance did the girls take any photos of you in that awful dress?

W: No, not that I am aware of, but just for the record: There is no such thing as organized crime!

D: Good answer.

The Tea Party Girls

The Mortgage Crisis (let me get this straight)

So a banker guy who drives a BMW gave a subprime mortgage that he wasn't supposed to so he could make a commission to pay for his country club dues to a guy who drives a Ford Pinto who wanted to have a life style like the guy in the BMW but couldn't afford the interest rate on a home he shouldn't have been buying in the first place, sold by a real estate agent driving a leased Cadillac who priced the house to high to begin with further driving up the cost of a already over inflated housing market. (That was just the longest sentence I ever wrote). This was done millions of times, sold in triple A rated bundles on the stock market to the rest of the world with no checks or balances.

So how does this affect me you ask, Mr. already paid for his house, not in the stock market? Well for one thing, your parent's life savings 401K plan has been wiped in half, so forget any inheritance. Also the Butcher, the Baker and the Candlestick Maker that live in your community will be closing their shop doors being that they have no business due to the fact that their customers have no jobs or extra cash to spend. Your community is looking pretty bleak and I haven't even mentioned the up and coming rise in violent and petty crime.

So the next time you're at a stop light with your squeegee and Windex bottle and you see a BMW pull up, you may just want to ask for the money first before anything gets started.

Letter to My Publisher

Wilson (W): Todd, will you please write a letter to my publisher for me, my paws are sore and I want to inquire why I haven't received royalties in awhile? Ready? Ok, Dear Pig F*****

Todd (T): Hey, you can't start off a letter like that, there are rules and conventions. Who are you writing to anyway, Rush Limbaugh?

W: No, I said my publisher.

T: Well how about starting off with Dear Sir?

W: Ok, Dear Sir Pig F*****

T: Wo, wo, wo. I'm not writing that.

Daisy (D): Will you two quiet down in here I can't hear my favourite TV show "Every Dog has its Day".

W: Who's on for today?

D: Dr. Phil. They're going to castrate Dr. Phil so his genes don't get passed on to future generations: A high price to pay for being a hack and giving bad diagnoses. Imagine, telling parents that their little boy is going to be like Jeffrey Dahmer because he exhibits two behaviours out of six required for a full diagnoses of psychopath (usually reserved for politicians and bankers), just for TV ratings. I think Dr. Phil has three himself if you include bulling.

W: Oh I've got to watch, this is going to be good. So Todd, write that letter for me.

T: I'm not writing that letter!

The Road Too Much Traveled: The Interview

Interviewer (I): So I hear your going off the beaten track?

Wilson T. (T): Yea, this road is too much traveled.

(I): Some say the East.

(T): Some are wrong aren't they? No the East is filled with power hungry kooks who want to manipulate and control the people and the natural resources, along with the sheep that mindlessly follow them. I don't know who I can't stand more, not to mention the bizarre dogmatic delusional belief systems that are taught and learned to govern their culture. Talk about abusing the human spirit!

(I): What on earth are you talking about?

T: Come on? As soon as I step foot in any a number of those states, I have to look a certain way, act a certain way and believe a certain way or I am breaking some made up religious commandment, all a rouse to control and manipulate the population.

Again not to mention also having to deal with the droids who already buy into the rules and regulations. They don't like when you point out how thru propaganda they have become indoctrinated. How illogical, irrational and delusional they are. They are a violent people.

I: It's the same here in the USA.

T: I was talking about the USA; I haven't even left for the East yet!

I: Well, the common man need rules and regulations to follow so he can feel safe, then his perception and interpretation of the world will make sense to himself.

T: What a crock! So how come all men aren't equal?

I: In essence they are. Though in order for life to flow easily there has to be some designation of duties. For instance we need our garbage collected. We elect civil officials, pay them so they can put up with the responsibility. We need police for the people who forget the rules that we all agreed upon through the democratic process of voting. Take craping for instance. If a guy takes a crap on your lawn are you going to shoe him away? No, that is what the police are for, whom you pay with your tax dollars. If you don't like the set up, you vote to change the status quo. Now in dictatorships you are

	the sheep and the ruling class just kills you if you make waves.
T:	Ok, I get it. If the dictatorship is really sophisticated and hidden, it will insulate itself within layers upon layers of customs and rules and beliefs and ideology. This intern allows each social class to govern and manipulate its' own. This allowing the small ruling class to control and stay in power. Occasionally there are bribes and large cash payments called stock options.
I:	I see, forever trying to keep up with and be like "The Jones". Certain cultural norms and morays, a high bar so to speak for everything under the sun: from social graces and manners to genuflecting at the altar of their choice. All this busyness keeps the wandering heard occupied from questioning the real balance of power. The 1% still controls 95% of the world's wealth and the planets' destruction.
T:	So now you know why I'm fed up and going off the beaten track.
I:	Yes, where was that again Wilson T.?
T:	Well, take care got to go.

The Bus Trip: Go Greyhounds

Daisy (D): Wilson I was really looking forward to our bus tour of the inbred slack-jawed bucktoothed hillbillies of the deep South, and those are just the politicians but after your first book I don't think were welcomed in the States of Louisiana, Mississippi, Alabama, Arkansas, Oklahoma, and parts of Texas.

Wilson (W): Do you really care? This is a demographic that will buy Tide just because it's on their favorite NASCAR drivers' side-panel.

D: Well, I wanted to see upfront what an indoctrinated, hypnotized consumer looks like.

W: Listen, don't be bad mouthing Tide. I don't mind the population of six States after us but don't be stirring up a corporate giant like Tide. You do remember that big business did rape and kill Catholic nuns via the rebels backed by middle management: our own Government in Central America in the 1980's to squelch the peoples uprising for Democracy. What better way to sell their agenda than to use a grade B actor: enter President Regan. If Corporate America does not get its way, you're a dead man, or delegated to the third world.

D: I still want to go on a bus trip. I was hoping to beat up on the politically-correct, I didn't vote for them! They changed the word cripple to: motivationally challenged. Then they changed the word midget to: the stratospherically challenged and or: the super small giants.

W: You got to be kidding, what idiots.

D: You can't use the word idiot, there called: the perceptional challenged to common sense phenomenally subjective awareness.

W: Good grief. Ok, how about us visiting the great Historic Brothels and Bordellos of Mid-West America?

D: You're not going to start off with any of your low-brow wacky high-jinx are you?

W: Absolutely not my precious little desert flower, I'd thought we'd go for strictly historical reasons only, maybe shake a few hands.

D: Well I don't know, it sounds a little corny to me. I'd say we try somewhere else first for starters. How about a tour of the rusted out dilapidated cities of the North where a lot of minorities live? We could see firsthand poor

The Bus Trip: Go Greyhounds 131

people and all their behavioral problems. Think of the many that have fallen thru the cracks of society's safety net?

W: You mean the middle-class? That's too depressing, besides who else is going to hold your towel for you at the country club?

D: There are too many poor with no food and a culture to self-absorbed to care, there is not enough of a middle-class to support the rich.

W: Sure there is, how about the rest of the world?

D: You mean America becomes a third world country, a smelly smoldering heap of huddled masses?

W: Exactly, that is why we should start off with a tour of the rich gated communities of the West. Think of it! Swimming pools, movie stars, black gold, California green tea, the Beverly Hillbillies. We'll start off with the rich supporting us.

D: This is not the meaning of our lives and what we are doing in this incarnation you know! The Greek philosopher Socrates once said: A life unexamined is not worth living!

W: Well the German philosopher Nietzsche examined his life and committed suicide.

D: Those German philosophers never had a sense of humor. So are you going to examine and introspect?

W: Yes, but what better way to contemplate the alleviation of human suffering while relaxing in a swimming pool.

GOD

Daisy (D): Wilson do you believe in God?

Wilson (W): Of course. Dog, God, call it what you will, there is definitely an Infinite creative intelligence to the universe. Think of it, of all the trillions and zillions of snowflakes no two are alike. How about all the hundreds of billions of planets and galaxies? How about the miracle of childbirth, music, laughter? Yes there is definitely a God.

D: Do you believe in religion?

W: Not for me, but it is a wonderful thing for the many as long as a religion does not control and manipulate the congregation. Think of a priest or minister as a master of ceremonies' to help guide the party along to a happy conclusion or comforting understanding. People need to make sense of certain events in their lives and religion fills that need by putting meaning and significance to any particular event. Take Baptisms: the welcoming into the family of mankind. Marriage: the union of two into one. These all have deeply profound spiritual cosmic life changing significance. You need a guide, a mediator, a master of ceremonies if you will. Take Death: the passing from one plane of existence to another, this is intensely sad for the loved ones who are left behind, especially if the dearly departed is a child. This brings up questions of WHY. Are you going to answer these while your grieving, crying? This is why High Priests come in handy, and religion does serve a purpose that helps mankind, as long as that religion does not oppress the congregation or make the women walk behind the men all covered up, or is not backed by a political agenda, the confectionary industry or the Central Banking System.

D: So why don't you join a religion and celebrate the wonder of it all?

W: I can celebrate the wonder of it all without joining a religion. Right now before you rudely interrupted me I was appreciating this beautiful sunset. Come join me and experience Gods wonder first hand. We don't need a religious festival throwing around brightly colored chalk to celebrate the sunset. Let's just celebrate the sunset by actually partaking and looking at the sunset.

D: What about all the other people?

W: If any of the myriad of religious ceremonies comfort and help the humans understand this world then this is a good thing. I hurt

	when humans suffer; I like to see them happy.
D:	I still don't understand why we don't join a religion, maybe one with doggie treats and no rolled up newspapers.
W:	Because we can't, were dogs. Dogs don't join religions, were not even allowed to.
D:	Well why the hell didn't you say that in the first place, wasting my time with such concepts, I missed the sunset for cryn-out-loud!
W:	YOU know, you're really getting on my nerve.

Being Enlightened Doesn't Play Well in The Suburbs

Daisy (D): Wilson dear, if someone who is fairly well read, well versed in culture, history, all the arts, math and sciences, all the mystics and religions, for them to say that "they know nothing", wouldn't appear too extreme, actually quite humbling wouldn't you think? For someone to know much and still know that he doesn't know, right?

Wilson (W): Yes, It's kind of like Carl Sandburg at the end of his life likening himself to an innocent child playing on the beach, something to that affect.

D: Yes ok, so now if someone tells you that "they are nothing", you knowing full well that they have contemplated their existence within the enormous totality of the cosmos, that wouldn't appear extreme, would it? Conversely, the epiphany is of interconnectedness with everything.

W: No. I understand the awesome power of seeing ones insignificance, as a grain of sand on a vast beach is a metaphorical comparison of oneself in relation to the Universe.

D: So, with all that in mind, if someone comes up to you and says that they know nothing and are nothing, wouldn't you want to hang out with them?

W: No way! I'm no glutton for punishment. Those enlightened ones who see it all and are aware of it all in its totality are a drag to hang out with. They're always too serious. Most of the time, you find them wandering around outside bus stations mumbling to themselves. Well, for the few exceptions of madcap enlightened musicians and yogis in the 1960's who professed peace and love, those were fun times. Those folks had heart, they really knew how to party and have fun. Other than those wonderful few, people who say that they know nothing and are nothing, I generally try to avoid. It just doesn't play well in the suburbs. Now someone of substance, like Pamela Anderson, that's a human I really could sink my teeth into, literally and metaphorically.

D: You're kidding, right? Substance? Can't you get past that infantile developmental stage?

W: You're the one with nine nipples remember. You've been into Todd's damn library again, haven't you?

D: This isn't going to be like the time when you were single and tried to make the perfect female canine, where you attempted to combine the body speed of a Greyhound with the quick mind of a Poodle, the heart of a Labrador and the mystical savvy of a Saint Bernard is it Dr. Frankenstein?

W: No Daisy, You are Plato's divine pyramid personified, where beauty, wisdom and truth all come together as one glorious harmonic. You are that Universal message sent down from the heavens, crystallized, made manifest on Earth in every moment of time. Ok?

D: Good, I'm glad we got that straightened out! So tell me Wilson what is your next book that you are working on about?

W: The story is about a Boxer who's a boxer that moonlights as an insect exterminator.

D: Tell me about it.

W: Well, he exterminates the foulest, most heinous of insects. Yes, out dated modes of science and to rethink our technology to help our earth and of course Republicans.

D: He doesn't poison them, does he?

W: Of course not, he lets the light of truth evaporate their power.

D: Well what about the Boxer's boxing?

W: The Boxer never gives up the fight he always keeps swinging

THE END.

About Wilson and Daisy's Owner

Todd has a private psychotherapy practice. He is licensed in the State of New York and the Province of Ontario.

Living with two dogs that are anarchists, he feels that for the family's safety from government political oppression, it is paramount to have dual citizenship and residences in both countries.

Todd is encouraging Wilson to retire. Wilson and Daisy plan on running for political office.

To contact Wilson's owner and book information: jtg@live.ca

CPSIA information can be obtained
at www.ICGtesting.com
Printed in the USA
FSHW01n1848260418
47511FS